GAME CHANGER

HOT RUGBY KNIGHTS - BOOK ONE

COURTNEY CLARK MICHAELS

AUGUST PUBLISHING

Game Changer
Hot Rugby Knights-Book One
Finn's Story

by Courtney Clark Michaels

This book is a work of fiction. Names, characters, places and incidents are the product of the author's imagination or are used fictitiously. Any resemblance to actual events, locales, or persons, living or dead, is coincidental.

Cover Design - Melville Design

For Manaia, Niko, AJ and Amira.
My game changers.

This book contains depiction of the following: stalking, parental infidelity, home invasion.

Every effort has been made by the author to handle this content with sensitivity, however please consider whether this may be upsetting for you as a reader and take care of yourself.

CHAPTER 1

It was as hot as Hades' ballsack.

The unforgiving January sun blazed down on the field as Finn Chalmers collapsed across the touchline and rolled onto his back, dragging air into his lungs.

"Too much pavlova over the holidays, eh?" Manu Esera asked, from a metre away, as if he wasn't in exactly the same position.

"I only had one," Finn gasped.

"Family-size?"

"Fuck you, man. It's the only dessert I can have at Christmas."

"Poor little coeliac."

Finn grunted. It didn't matter he'd been playing league for twenty years now, shuttle runs never got easier. He concentrated on breathing in through his nose. *Sweet, sweet oxygen.* His lungs burned, as did the indignity, because despite Manu's teasing, the two of them had been back in the Auckland Knights' training facility since Boxing Day preparing for the upcoming season, but today was the first day of preseason training and the first time they'd laid eyes on the

1

others since their defeat in the grand final last year. Either his teammates had worked out elsewhere during their summer vacation, or they'd enjoyed a longer break than Finn and Manu.

He got his answer within the next minute as more bodies crossed the line and joined them on the grass, groans filling the air.

If this was how he felt, he could only imagine the pain of the men who'd overindulged.

"Right, you lot." Brian 'Harro' Harrington barked, the rolled 'R' pronunciation of his Southland accent doing nothing to soften his words. Their head coach was the epitome of the stereotypical grizzled man from New Zealand's South Island, but he was also a legend of the game and a coaching icon. Finn had grown up watching Harro on TV in the common room of his boarding house, and he felt the need to pinch himself now and then that one of his heroes was part of the fabric of his everyday life.

"You did okay today," Harro told them when they gathered around him, several players bent at the waist, recovering. "Wasn't great, but wasn't terrible either. I know we wish last season had gone a different way-" there was a pause as they acknowledged their loss. They'd hoped for a back-to-back championship run after their success two years ago- "but we've got to make sure we leave that in the past. We've got a couple of new players, and we're looking forward to the upcoming season."

Harro cleared his throat, becoming preoccupied with the tablet in his hands. "On the subject of new beginnings, Matt Hollis has indicated he won't be available for captaincy this year." Surprise pricked at the base of Finn's neck. Hollis had been their captain for four years, ever since Finn arrived at the Knights. He shot the big blond man a look, but Hollis stared straight ahead, not looking at anyone, the line of his jaw tight. Finn returned his attention to Harro as he continued. "We'll be looking for someone else to lead us into battle each week, someone who can do the team justice, represent us well and protect our interests, on the field and off. The coaching staff and I will watch you over the next few weeks, and we'll rotate a few people into the position for the preseason games. So, pull your heads in and make sure you're only sticking out for the right reasons." Harro nodded sharply. "That's it then. Bugger off. I'll see you tomorrow."

They made their way slowly across the field, Finn and Manu at the back of the pack.

"Surprise about Hollis," Finn muttered under his breath as the rest of the team disappeared into the shadows of the tunnel leading to the changing rooms.

"Yeah," Manu answered thoughtfully. "Did you hear anything from him over the holidays?"

"Nothing," Finn replied.

Manu and Hollis didn't get on well – their captain had been rude to Manu's wife Clare the first time they met and despite the Pacific Islander's easy-going nature, he took any slight against his woman seriously.

"Hope he's laid off the booze," Manu said, his voice sombre. "It's not doing him any favours."

Finn nodded. Alcohol was an unpredictable mistress at the best of times for pro athletes, and a paparazzi shot of Hollis passed out drunk in a gutter had made the rounds after their last finals loss. Nothing disastrous, but those in the Knights' team had seen him in similar states a few too many times during away games over the last year. Combined with rumours his marriage was under strain, the loss of the captaincy could be a chance for him to get his head on straight or lose it completely.

"What are you and Cara up to tonight?" Manu asked over the clatter of steel on concrete as they made their way through the tunnel. "Do you want to come with us and win a bar tab at quiz night?" Manu and Clare lived down the road from a pub that ran quizzes on Tuesday nights, and they took the competition seriously.

Finn's heart leapt at the mention of Cara, and he cursed the organ. Would it ever behave itself when it heard her name? Finn Chalmers had been in love with Cara Holt since the day he met her five years ago, and for five years he'd been firmly relegated to the role of her best friend. *We are best friends,* he reminded himself.

Certainly there was nobody else with whom he spent so much time, nobody else who saw him with his guard down, sprawled on his couch in sweats and sniffling at Disney animated films. Nobody else suffused his entire being with a warm sense of rightness, like molten gold flowing outwards from his heart through his bloodstream every time he saw her. Nobody else tugged at his chest and left a void in his stomach when they left, the way Cara had the first time she walked away from him after their first Educational Pedagogy tutorial at university and every time since. Nobody else left him with a disconcerting twitch under his skin - *touch her, tell her, she's yours* - and the corresponding ache that weighed down his limbs when she chatted away to him about failed dates, or even worse, successful ones.

"Hey." Fingers snapped in front of his face. "You okay?"

Finn looked down at Manu, who sat on the bench in front of his locker, unlacing his boots. "Yeah, I'm good."

"Dreaming of all those ladies lined up waiting for you to text them, huh, Charming?" Rangi Katu passed by them, a towel slung across his shoulder, heading for the showers. "We should all be so lucky." The young Māori player slapped Finn on the shoulder.

Finn forced a gravel-like laugh out of his throat. "Not exactly."

Manu was watching him closely. "So…quiz?"

"I'll ask Cara when I get home," Finn promised. He moved a couple of stations along to his own locker as the instrumental strains of Beyonce and The Chicks' *Daddy Lessons* remix rang out. "Or I'll ask her now," he muttered, pulling his phone from the top shelf and swiping to answer the call.

"Hey. Are you up for a quiz with the Eseras tonight?"

"Finn." Cara's voice trembled and every molecule in his body pulled tight at the fear laced through her tone.

Goosebumps rose on his skin, the hair lifted at the back of his neck and the words burst out of him. "Are you alright? What happened?" The surrounding chatter lessened, but he barely noticed, reaching for his bag and rifling through it for street shoes.

"I'm okay," she assured him quickly, and he could almost see her there, with her copper hair and big brown eyes, talking him down from the ledge of panic. "I'm fine. It's just, I've been getting notes at work. A few of them. And this morning, before I left home, there was one on my car."

"You're being *stalked*?" His voice echoed loudly through the now-quiet room, nobody speaking, nobody moving, the soft rain of the showers in the background the only noise. From the corner of his eye, Finn saw Manu move towards him and he shot a hand out to halt the bigger man's progress while he listened.

"More like being harassed, I think, but Denise wants me to call the police -" *Thank you, Denise* "-and I wondered if you could be here while I talk to them?"

"Yes." He was moving now, phone tucked under his ear as he stood on one foot, ripping off his boot.

"I know you have training, so it's fine if you can't-"

"Cara," Finn interrupted, pushing the red mist of rage aside so he could talk without bellowing, without scaring her further. "Call the police. I'll be there by the time they arrive. Are you at work?"

"Yes," her voice was small, the shield of bravery slipping.

"Do not move. Lock yourself in the office. I'll be there in twenty minutes." It was a thirty-minute drive on a good day. Both boots off now, he shoved them in his bag and whipped the zip up without pulling his street shoes out. He could drive in socks.

"Thanks, Finn."

He hung up, heart racing.

"Cara?" Manu asked tightly, and Finn managed a sharp nod.

"I've got to go." He was already moving towards the door, the eyes of his teammates tracking him. Cara had come with him to the Knights, a package deal. She sat in the team box with the WAGs at every home game, attended their fundraisers, prize givings, hell, even their pizza nights. Their palpable concern for her followed him all the way to the carpark.

He made the drive in record time and burst through the front door of the well-maintained wooden villa that functioned as a preschool, in time to see two people in suits make their way into the office to the right of the hallway lined with colourful school bags. He followed them in, finding Cara standing in the middle of the light-drenched room shaking their hands.

"Cara." Instinct drove him towards her and he wrapped her in his arms, inhaling the familiar scent of raspberry body lotion and the silky press of her hair against his cheek until one of the cops cleared their throat behind him.

Standing back, he searched her eyes, and she offered him a wobbly smile before turning her attention to the others in the room.

"Detective Pring, Detective Maxwell, this is Finn. He's here in a support capacity."

Detective Pring, a stocky Asian man, nodded briskly at Finn, as did his short white female partner, although her eyes betrayed a hint of zealous fandom behind her stoic expression. *A Knights supporter.*

Finn kept his hand on Cara's back as she offered beverages that were rebuffed, until they sat in a distorted circle of rolling desk chairs.

"Why don't you start at the beginning?" Detective Maxwell said, and Cara's careful intake of breath echoed in the small space.

"Our summer break ended last week. The second day back, I went out to my car after work and there was a note under my windshield. I thought it was a parking ticket or a flyer at first, but when I opened it, it said, 'I like your hair down'. I thought perhaps it was from one of my co-workers, or a random act of kindness, but there have been two more since then. This morning when I was at home about to leave for work, I saw another one on my windshield. I came to work and asked around. It's not one of the other staff members."

Finn's gut tightened with every word and he folded his arms, jamming his hands into his armpits to keep from lashing out in fear and frustration.

Two weeks. For two weeks, some psycho has left her notes, and she hasn't mentioned them. They messaged almost daily, saw each other at least twice a week.

"Why didn't you say something?" he muttered, low and angry, interrupting Detective Maxwell's confirmation of Cara's home address.

"I get a lot of notes," Cara explained patiently. She gestured to a small pile of papers on the long wooden desk in the shared office. "I've already had three others today, and it's only ten in the morning."

Detective Pring picked them up and Finn wheeled his

chair closer to read over his elbow as he flipped through them.

Cara + Georgie. The first piece of paper was decorated with what looked like a flower and a pair of stick figures with Freddy Kruger-esque fingers, the writing huge and loose in the way kids wrote when they copied letters. That was par for the course. He'd seen a thousand similar notes in her bag and scattered across her kitchen counter since she'd started teaching.

The second one was on personalised stationery, a pink stylised 'S' at the top of the lined paper. *Miss Holt, please refrain from teaching the children Bollywood dances. Some of those movements are extremely inappropriate for their age. I will mention this to your supervisor.* Detective Pring held it up with a questioning look, and Cara shrugged.

"Georgie's mum. A Karen by nature, if not by name."

The third, an orange Post-it, decorated with a smiley face, contained another scrawled message.

Oh my god, Cara. Georgie's mum hates you. I bet her head explodes during your Pride Month activities.

"That's from my supervisor, Denise," Cara supplied.

"Do you have the note from your car this morning?" Detective Pring asked, the first words he'd spoken so far. Cara reached into her bag and pulled out a folded piece of paper, handing it across. The detective unfolded it; the heavy cream stationery out of place amongst the piles of white printer paper or coloured card that decorated the rest of the office. Inside, five words in bold, precise penmanship.

You are a special woman.

"That's creepy as fuck." The words were out before he could stop them, and he regretted them the instant Cara sucked in her breath. Scooching his chair towards her, Finn wrapped his arm around her shoulders. She looked at him gratefully, leaning on him as she answered the detectives' questions. It took almost an hour, going over details and schedules, asking about any enemies or suspicious behaviour, romantic entanglements gone wrong and her relationships with the three other women she lived with in her Epsom flat.

Eventually, the questioning wound up, and they moved to the useless advice portion of the visit. *Have someone walk you to your car. Buy a whistle. Lock your doors.*

"Hang on," Finn interrupted. "You can't seriously expect her to go home? This arsehole knows where she lives."

"There's not much we can do about that," Detective Maxwell said, standing. "She'll have to be careful and hopefully this person will lose interest or reveal themselves. It could simply be a secret admirer working up some nerve. We'll look into it, of course, but without more evidence there's not much we can do at this stage."

Cara touched his arm briefly. "It's okay, Finn. I'll talk to the girls when I get home and we'll work out a plan."

"The hell you will," Finn snapped. "You're not going home again except to get your stuff."

"Finn." Cara moved closer, lowering her voice. "I can't afford a hotel, and I won't let you pay for one either," she added quickly.

"You're not going to a hotel. You're moving in with me."

"I most certainly am not." The words flew from Cara's mouth instinctively.

Finn's chest puffed up further, his broad shoulders almost filling the office. "Cara," he began, his voice low and dangerous, the way it got when she mentioned walking alone at night or online dating. "This is not up for debate."

"It's my life, Finnegan," she replied, and he winced at the use of his hated full name. "There is no debate. I decide."

They were almost toe-to-toe now, and Finn bent his head to offset the mere two inches of height difference that separated them, his blue eyes fervent as he spoke again.

"Cara, someone is stalking you. They know where you live. Even if you take your safety out of the equation, staying at your flat might endanger the other women. You know how seriously I take security at my place. The cameras, the alarms. Right now, it's the best place you can be while the police have a chance to investigate further."

"It's not a bad idea." The quiet voice of Detective Pring interjected, and Cara wrenched her gaze away from Finn to look at him. Honestly, she'd forgotten the cops were still there. "You say you have security?" Pring was looking at Finn now, who straightened and nodded.

"I live on the North Shore in a semi-rural gated community. On top of the communal security precautions, my place has ten feet high fences and alarms, with top-of-the-line sensor lights and cameras. Beach access is through a built-in door with a security code."

Detective Pring let out a low whistle. "Pretty heavy security for a sportsman."

Beside her, Finn stiffened. "Safety is important to me."

The detective nodded before refocusing his attention on Cara. "It's up to you, of course, Ms Holt, but if I were you, I'd consider your boyfriend's offer. It sounds like he's got the means to stop anyone accessing your car outside of work hours, and staying away from home might throw them off enough that they give up."

"He's not my boyfriend," Cara said absently, turning the idea of staying at Finn's over in her head.

"Even so," Detective Pring said. "It sounds like you might be better off at his place for a while. We'll be in touch." He handed each of them a card with his details on, then nodded and departed, trailed by his partner and the heart-eyes she'd been shooting at Finn since he walked in.

"Finn-" Cara began again, but he cut her off.

"I know what you're going to say, Cara, but listen. I know." She bet he did too. Nobody knew her better than Finn, with maybe the exception of her little sister, but Izzy was currently in Toulon, or maybe Barcelona, and even if Cara had any intention of mentioning this situation to her - which she certainly did not - she was unlikely to be much help anyway. Cara had always handled any problems that came up while Izzy flitted through life like a runaway butterfly.

"I'm not your responsibility," Cara managed. "I can take care of myself. I can," she protested at the look he gave her.

"It's not a matter of being taken care of, Cara." Finn's brow rumpled, an adorable little divot in the middle of that flawless, sun-kissed skin that made him one of the most popular bachelors in Auckland. "It's your safety. I can offer you a level of safety you can't get at home, or even at a hotel, for that matter. And as for caring about you? Don't pretend I shouldn't, because we both know I do. You're the most important person in my life."

Sighing, Cara nodded. "I know. You're my best friend too. We'd be having this same argument if the situation was reversed." She rested her forehead against his shoulder, closed her eyes and inhaled. Underneath the vinegary-clean scent of sweat from his training session hung the unique blend of fresh-cut grass and Dolce and Gabbana that never failed to calm her. *Finn.*

"Thanks for coming," she mumbled into his Knights' training top, and he wrapped one big arm around her back, his hand settling on her hip.

"Anytime," he said into her hair, and she smiled at the warm puff of his breath against her scalp.

They stood like that for a minute, maybe a few seconds longer, where she let herself truly feel the fear and anxiety she'd been battling since she'd spotted the note on her car window this morning; let it flood her bloodstream and roll across her skin before she began the process of rebuilding her defences. She focused on her breathing first, dragging oxygen deep and low, the tang of Finn's scent making it harder to focus, but she managed. Then, opening her eyes, stepping out of his comfortable embrace, and finally pulling her loose hair to the side and braiding it, securing her work with the hair elastic that was almost permanently around her wrist.

Finn watched her the whole time, blue eyes dark under his frown. "Better?"

"I will be." She shot him a small smile, but a genuine one, and his shoulders ticked down. "I need to speak to Denise about leaving early today and work out what to pack from my place. If you're sure about me staying with you…"

"I'm sure."

"I'll pay you board." Even now, with all the other things she had to worry about, her meagre bank balance danced in the front of her mind.

"You will not."

"Finn…"

"Think of it as an extended sleepover. Besides, the cops could catch this person tomorrow and I'd have to work out a refund."

Cara huffed out a reluctant smile.

"I'll come now and get settled. I won't be any good to the kids at the moment."

He nodded. "I'll wait here while you talk to Denise, then

follow you back to yours and wait while you pack before we head home."

It was a wise move. Last time Finn had entered the central workspace of the preschool, he'd been mobbed by tiny fans and forced into reading *Princess Smartypants* and *How Maui Slowed the Sun* to a mat full of awed kids. Plus a couple of awed teachers.

True to his word, he waited patiently in the office while she filled her boss in on the police's visit and their suggestion she stay with Finn, then followed her home. He insisted on going into her house first and checking things out before allowing her in to pack clothes, toiletries and other necessities into the large Auckland Knights sports bag Finn had gifted her his first season with the team.

Finn's black BMW wagon with tinted windows trailed the crappy little red Corolla Cara had owned since high school across the Harbour Bridge, all the way to his gated community, backing onto a marine reserve with views stretching out across the Hauraki Gulf, shimmering sapphire in the midday sun.

Finn's house had always intimidated her, with the large columns crafted from Otago schist out front and soaring cathedral ceilings and gleaming wooden floors inside. It was a home meant for a family, but Finn moved around it in almost silence. She could count on one hand the number of times she'd heard music playing through the in-home speakers outside of team get-togethers.

She pulled up to the spot she usually parked in, by the hydrangea hedge heavy with blue blooms separating the gravel driveway from the wide rolling lawn area. Before she'd managed to open her door, Finn was there, helping her out, grabbing her bag from the boot of her car and leading her to the wide front doors, punching in the code to enter.

"Do you want this in your room?" He hefted the bag on his shoulder.

"Yes, please."

"Go make yourself a cup of tea. I'll be there in a sec."

True to his word, he joined her in the kitchen before the kettle had finished boiling, wrapping one thick arm around her as she stared unseeingly at the tea selection box he kept on the counter as if this was a fancy bed and breakfast.

"You good?"

"Nope."

His arm tightened.

"What can I do?"

"You're doing it."

The kettle switched off and he moved away to fix a peppermint tea in her favourite mug, the big red one that was wider at the base than the top.

She followed him into the living area quietly, settling into her usual position on the fawn leather couch and letting Finn cover her legs in a blanket despite the blazing sun outside.

They sat in silence while she sipped her drink, cradling the mug in her hands and letting the warmth of the tea, the blanket and the summer's day outside sink into her bones and wash away the chill that had settled there the moment she saw the rectangle of paper tucked under her windshield wiper that morning. Finn laid back with his head on the armrest, his bare feet brushing the edges of her blanket and closed his eyes, the flexing of his left ankle where he harboured an old injury the only sign he was still awake.

"Okay," Cara said, as she drained the last of her tea. "I'm ready to talk."

He sat up immediately, blue eyes intent on her. "Let's hear it."

"What the fuck?" Cara cried. "How does someone think this is appropriate behaviour? If it's a wooing technique, it's sorely misplaced. Just walk up to a person and tell them you like them instead of being a complete creep. Why on Earth would this be considered seductive? And why me? There's nothing special about me." Finn opened his mouth like he might disagree, but she carried on without letting him speak. "And what if it's not some misguided secret admirer? What if it's an intimidation technique? It's working, but I'm angry about it. They think they can intimidate me? *Me?* They can go fuck themselves."

Finn let her rant for a while, murmuring his agreement until she ran out of steam, then ordered pizza from the upmarket pizzeria in the nearest suburb and put on *Meet the Robinsons*. They spent the rest of the afternoon in comfortable silence. *Turning Red* followed *Meet the Robinsons* and Cara slowly relaxed. Before the six o'clock news had finished her eyes were drooping, and he escorted her to the second floor bedroom she used whenever she stayed over and told her to wake him in the night if she needed anything - *anything,* he stressed - before leaving her to change into the Knights t-shirt she wore to bed and snuggle into the fresh sheets.

No doubt about it. Finn was the best friend a girl could have.

CHAPTER 2

"*L*ooking a bit tubby there, Charming."

"Can't help it." Finn snapped. "Every time I fuck your wife she bakes me a cake."

Hollis looked taken aback. "Steady on, mate."

Finn glared at him and strode into the weights room. It was an arsehole thing to say, not least because Manu had texted him last night to check on Cara and confirm that, according to Rangi Katu, Hollis' wife had kicked him out right after New Year's, but he felt like shit. The cramps had started last night twenty minutes after he finished the pizza that had definitely not been the gluten-free one he'd ordered. Now he was the saddest coeliac this side of the Bombay Hills, his stomach distended, pain shooting through him every time he moved. But it wasn't like he could skip the second training of the year, especially not now the captaincy was up for grabs.

His fight with Cara this morning hadn't helped either. He'd been horrified to find her in the kitchen, freshly showered, dressed for work and digging into his homemade muesli stash.

"What do you think you're doing?" he'd exploded.

"Eating breakfast?" she replied.

"Not that. Why are you wearing that?"

She'd glanced down at her cardigan, embroidered with her preschool's name and covering most of her summery dress. "Because they're my work clothes."

"You can't seriously intend on going to work today."

Ten minutes later, she'd stormed out of the kitchen, her accusations of Finn being a 'high-handed arsehole' ringing in his ears. And she'd taken his container of muesli with her.

He was still stewing over her foolishness as he threw himself onto the stretching mats next to Manu.

"How's it going?" the big prop asked.

Finn grunted in response. What could he say? He was so scared that fear threatened to choke him every time he thought about someone harming Cara? That knowing some obsessed stranger had her home address had his stomach roiling more than the gluten pizza base? That he'd cried with relief in the shower last night knowing she was safe in his house behind the best security measures money could buy?

"That good, huh?" Manu stretched into downward dog. "And Cara?"

"Stubborn."

Manu laughed. "The best ones always are."

"It's not funny," Finn gritted out. "She could get hurt. She went to work today. What if this guy doesn't back off? That's exactly where he'd expect her to be."

"It's a guy?"

"I'm assuming."

Manu sighed and transitioned to cobra. Finn rolled over and mirrored him, breathing deep into his abdomen in a way he hadn't managed since his phone rang in the changing room yesterday.

"I know you care about Cara," Manu cut him a meaningful look Finn pretended not to see. "But you have to respect her too. If she feels she can keep herself safe at work, that's her decision."

"I don't have to like it."

"It's pretty clear you don't, but if I've learnt anything about women, it's that they're not interested in hearing what men have to say about how they should conduct themselves."

Finn inclined his head slightly. Manu had a whip-smart wife, a force of nature for a sister and a terrifyingly efficient sister-in-law. Any insight he had into the female psyche was miles more than Finn had scraped together as an only child shunted off to an all-boys boarding school at eleven.

"Wanting to keep her safe seems like something she should be on board with."

"Sometimes the things that seem simplest cause the most friction."

Finn huffed out a small laugh. "Okay, Doctor Love."

"Relationship guru, I am," Manu replied in his Yoda voice. "Look at Hollis," he continued in his normal Pacific Island accent as they changed positions. "I bet whatever finally made Lauren wise up and kick him out started out small. A few drinks after a game with the boys, or a fan who posted a selfie standing a little too close. Now he's down a wife and we're down a captain."

"Who do you think Harro's looking at for it?" Finn worked to keep his voice casual as he leant into a hamstring stretch. The situation with Cara had whipped his focus from Harro's announcement yesterday, but fuck he wanted it.

The extra income assigned to the captaincy was a bonus, of course - he could funnel it directly into his monthly charity donations - but more than that, the prestige associated with the position called to him. A siren song lapping at the edges of his mind, full of promises of validation. Something to show he'd made the right call going into professional sports rather than the path laid out for him by generations of conservative, white ancestors.

His parents certainly didn't think so, but perhaps holding the title of captain would stop their pained expressions every month when they enquired about his work. Their current dismay ate at his gut every time. Anyone watching their exchanges would assume his line of work involved human trafficking rather than a tame underwear endorsement modelling campaign for the pride his parents showed in his chosen career.

"Not sure," Manu admitted. "Zac had a good season last year, and he's really coming into his own. Victor has the mana and the experience, for sure." He shot Finn a quick look. "You interested?"

Finn shrugged. "Maybe."

"Have you got time for captain duties?" A voice came from behind them. "Not going to cut into your romancing at all?"

Finn cut a look over his shoulder. "You're one to talk, Dom. I've seen your girlfriend's social media. Rose petals and champagne. I've got nothing on you for romance."

Dominic McQueen grinned easily, running a big hand through his flowing blonde locks. Dom was new to the Knights this season, a huge shaggy bear of a man, but Finn had played with him in academy teams on his way up and they'd always got on well.

"When she's worth the effort, lad, you'll make it happen."

Finn gritted his teeth. Effort wasn't his problem. His problem was that his heart was already spoken for. Now and then, when Cara was in a relationship, he dated. The rules were simple. One time per woman. No expectations, no strings. It was easier that way. Any more and the risk of them developing feelings he couldn't return was too high. He didn't want to lead anyone on, but he got lonely occasionally. The vast majority of his dates ended with a chaste kiss goodnight, occasionally more, and thanks for a pleasant evening. Unfortunately, there'd been enough of them during the past five years, combined with the ridiculous nickname he'd acquired from his shoot for ESPN's Body issue a couple of years back - the Prince Charming of Rugby League - his reputation as some kind of Casanova far surpassed reality, even in his teammates' eyes. The one time he'd attempted a relationship, it had fizzled out within three months. Natalie was gorgeous; intelligent, driven, a competitive gymnast. But despite her wonderful qualities and his desperate desire to move on from his unrequited crush on Cara, Finn hadn't summoned anything deeper than friendship for her and they'd parted on good terms.

He couldn't do anything about his reputation or his unrequited love for his best friend. God knows he'd tried with the latter, and as for the former? Well, maybe if he could return to the ESPN shoot, he'd reconsider posing naked save for a strategically placed game ball. But the captaincy? That he could manage. If only he could shrug off the unwelcome vision of himself as a good-time guy. That kind of reputation could easily turn both Harro and the public against him. Captains needed gravitas. A sense of responsibility and reliability, so players and spectators alike could count on them to do the right thing, have their teammates' backs and speak on their behalf. Finn pulled his right foot up behind him, stretching his quad muscle as determination flowed through him. If he wanted to be captain, he needed to rebrand himself as prime captaincy material. A hard man, tough and tenacious, stoic and steadfast. A man worthy of the position. Maybe then Cara would see another side of him. Maybe she'd see him as more than a friend.

~

"So you're staying with your friend? The pretty one from the rugby team?"

"Rugby league team," Cara corrected Magda, trying to look busy. Magda was, frankly, too old to still be teaching. She didn't like kids all that much, she refused to upskill to include new technological advances, and she microwaved fish in the preschool's small kitchen at least once a week. Cara was not a fan.

"Same thing, isn't it?"

"Not quite."

It would horrify Finn to think of his beloved rugby league being confused with rugby union. They might be similar in many regards and use almost identical balls, but he'd espoused the differences to her many times. Besides having fewer players, rugby league was, according to Finn, faster-paced, with harder tackles and more substitutions to keep the action going. The players' shorts were shorter, too. That was Cara's own observation though, one she hadn't voiced to Finn.

Finn, who had lost his damn mind at the idea of her going to work this morning.

Ridiculous.

She wasn't a superstar with a mansion and a savings account that most people could only dream of. She was a preschool teacher with a student loan who could only afford takeaway coffee twice a week. She was proud of her independence. Hell, after the way she'd grown up, she treasured it. It was bad enough that she was living in his house for now, but for him to expect her not to work? Not to have a source of income of her own? Anxiety dizzied her.

"Doesn't he live way out on the North Shore?" Magda's eyes lit up. "Does he have a pool?"

"No pool," Cara answered tightly, opening up the digital learning records and uploading images from this morning's scone-baking session with her students. Magda's question rankled. People always made assumptions about Finn, about his wealth, the underlying question of what they could get out of him colouring their interest no matter how hard they tried to disguise it. That he'd grown up wealthy only exacerbated it. It was one reason Cara was careful not to take advantage of his generous nature. They split payments for meals when they went out, took turns paying for rounds of drinks at the bar. She was determined to keep their friendship on a level playing field.

Even now, staying with him for the short term grated on her. It was one thing to stay the night after a few drinks or a *Lord of the Rings* marathon rather than returning to the city, but being a houseguest without a defined end date tilted her off balance. The thought of being indebted to anyone was disturbing enough, let alone Finn who was too polite to mention where she might inadvertently cross the line from staying out of need to taking advantage.

"The North Shore's lovely in summer," Magda mused, and Cara was saved from her fantasy of throwing the stapler at the older woman by the ringing of the phone.

"Hello?"

"Hi there, it's Bernard. I'm a bit early to pick up Georgie."

"Oh, perfect, we'll be out in a sec."

Cara hung up the phone. "I'm going to get Georgie ready for pickup," she murmured to Magda as she escaped the office.

She located Georgie, helped her with her shoes and bag and escorted her out to the gate where her father waited. Bernard Shaw was a slim white man, constantly focused on his phone, but Cara relished any time he was at drop-off or pick-up with Georgie because it gave her a reprieve from

Georgie's mother Lilith, a WASP-y, pinch-lipped woman with an almost physical aversion to Georgie learning about any culture other than her own.

Soleil's mum arrived next with bundles of white sage incense to gift to staff members, followed by Parker's German nanny with leftover pfeffernüsse cookies from the Christmas period and Cara was run off her feet facilitating pickups through the lunch period. When she finally got back to the office for her lunch break, she slumped in the spinny chair with a bowl of Finn's luxury muesli and checked her phone.

A photograph from Izzy of some European statue that looked suspiciously like an orgy, and a text from Finn.

Sorry about this morning. Please come to the stadium to see me when you finish work?

She sent him back a smiley face. He was a good man. He had been since she'd met him at uni when he was in the Knights' development squad, all fresh-faced and hopeful, and she was twenty-two, back at uni studying for her early childhood qualification after squeezing out the business degree her parents expected of her.

As much as this harassment unnerved her, it wouldn't scare her from living her life as she pleased. She'd spent too much of her life living around other people, their wants, their needs, too much time carving out her own identity and boundaries to have one unpleasant person shock her back into a life of anxious overthinking.

Denise popped her head into the office. "Are you okay in here?"

"Yup," Cara responded.

Denise entered and flopped into another chair. "These kids are off the wall today. Must be the pfeffernüsse."

"I looked up the recipe online," Cara said around her muesli. God, it was good. Miles better than the shitty generic stuff she bought on special from the bulk bins at the supermarket. "There's supposed to be molasses in it, plus the glaze on top. That's a year's worth of sugar for some of these kids."

"The three o'clock crash is going to be a nightmare," Denise groaned. "Did you see how proud Parker was to show her friends what she made though?"

"I know," Cara grinned. "It was so sweet. And she gave Ada the first one. They're the cutest little besties."

"How's your bestie?" Denise asked, leaning over to snag a protein ball out of the container they kept on the desk for emergency energy hits during paperwork sessions. "I thought he was going to stroke out yesterday."

"He's fine. He wanted me to stay home this morning though," Cara frowned.

"Yeah?" Denise eyed her. "I have to admit, I was expecting you to be absent."

"Why?" Defensiveness rang in Cara's tone. "Why should I let some weirdo stop me from living my life?"

"Whoa, whoa," Denise held up her hands, the tā moko tattoo on her hand almost blue in the early afternoon light. "I'm only saying, this can't be easy. It's okay if you need a little time to get yourself right. Manaakitanga, yeah?"

"I guess," Cara replied grudgingly. The Māori concept of extending respect, kindness and support to others was considered so important it was one of the founding principles of early childhood education in New Zealand, but it applied to everyone. "I feel uncomfortable relying on other people."

"No shame in needing help," Denise said mildly. "What would you tell a student?"

Cara rolled her eyes. "I'd say everyone needs friends to help them sometimes. Must you use the basic tenets of our work against me?"

Denise smirked. "Consider it professional development. Put it in your appraisal documents."

"You think that would hold up to the Teacher's Council?"

"Manaakitanga, babe." Denise winked at her as she leveraged out of her chair and headed towards the door. "Love always wins."

CHAPTER 3

Finn swung the Beemer into the Knights' Stadium's staff carpark and pulled up short at the sight of Cara standing in the Dumpster next to the player's entrance. He was out of the car like a shot, leaving the door open and the engine running.

"What the fuck do you think you're doing? Get out of there before you stab yourself with a needle!"

She rolled her eyes at him. "What kind of dodgy neighbourhood do you work in, Chalmers?" She bent over, the hem of her navy flowered dress fluttering around her knees as she reached for something he couldn't see.

"There you go." Her voice was a soft coo that wrapped around him and tugged at his heart and his balls. He'd gladly have savoured it if not for the current threat of hepatitis. She straightened again, holding something to her chest, and he caught a glimpse of cream fur and a sense of foreboding washed through him before she turned to him and he copped a good look at the ratty dog cradled in her arms.

"Isn't he sweet?"

No. No, no, no, no. This was not good. He loved his house.

He loved his unstained carpet and his fur-free couch and sleeping in without the threat of urine somewhere in his oasis of peace.

"No," he tried valiantly. "He's not sweet. He was in a Dumpster, for Christ's sake. He looks like hell and smells like death. Let's call the pound and they can find his owner."

"We're not calling the *pound*." Cara was aghast. "And we're certainly not returning him to whatever arsehole dumped him here. What is wrong with you? Here." She thrust the dog at him and he took it instinctively, holding it as far away from his body as he could while she clambered out of the Dumpster in a tangle of smooth limbs. Who stomped around inside Dumpsters?

"Give him here," she said, straightening up and brushing off her legs. Thank God she wore flat ankle boots. "I'll take him into the changing rooms for a shower while you park."

He tried to reason with her as she settled the animal in her arms, and it looked up at her as if she'd hung the moon. "Cara, he can't go in there."

Cara and the dog both stared at him silently, twin sets of imploring brown eyes doing nothing but pinning him under the weight of their combined plea.

Fuck.

He raked a hand through his hair. "Fine, but you tell no one, and you find him a new home as soon as possible. Yeah?"

Cara's grin split her face, happiness radiating out like a sunbeam and she bounced a little on the balls of her feet. "You're the best, Finn!" She reached up and pecked his cheek, the quick, soft press of her lips touching inside him and kick starting his heart. He reached past her to enter the door code. The scent of raspberries teased his nostrils, and he savoured the way her shoulder pressed against him, the curve of her cheek inches from his mouth.

"See you in there!"

With a sigh he strode back to his car, parked up properly, and headed inside. Cara was in a shower stall with the dog, sitting next to the spray zone, her dress ruched high on her thighs as she shampooed the canine with -

"Is that my shower gel?"

"Yup." She didn't even look up at him. "Now you two will smell the same. It'll help him bond with you."

"I don't want him to bond with me!" The scented bubbles swirling down the drain were the least of his concerns now. "I don't want a dog."

"You need one."

"I need a dog like I need a torn ACL." Finn reached behind him and tapped the doorframe as he said it. *Touch wood.*

"Fine. But we'll take him home tonight and give him some love. He needs it, poor thing. Imagine being tossed out like rubbish because some heartless person decided they didn't want you anymore?"

A piece of Finn's heart broke. *When she put it like that...he knew exactly how the dog felt.* And she'd called his place home.

"Only for tonight," he croaked. "And you clean up any mess he makes."

Cara beamed at him and he tried not to notice the way the spray had dampened the top half of her dress so it clung to her frame. "I will. I promise."

He let out another sigh and headed back to the main changing room, calling in an order to a butcher's shop near his house while he waited for Cara to finish up. It took a while, by the time she'd showered the pup and dried it with one of the built-in hairdryers, the dog quivering in pleasure as it leaned into the stream of warm air. When she was done, the dog looked significantly better, though no amount of luxury shower product could disguise the cream and caramel coloured blotches of fur that stuck out from his body like he'd been electrocuted. When Finn touched him, though, they were surprisingly soft, and the pup sniffed him curiously. He pulled his hand back at the wet touch of its nose to his hand and caught Cara smirking at him with a satisfied gleam in her eye.

"What?" Finn asked, but she only grinned.

"I'm going to name him Ted," she announced, scooping him up off the long counter and into her arms. "Come on, Ted. Time to go."

"One night," he called after them, but she ignored him, swishing through the changing room doors like a queen.

An hour later, he watched the pup scarfing down tiny cubes of steak from a brand new shiny red bowl in the corner of his kitchen. There was a water bowl too, all on a little mat to protect his floorboards. Cara sat at the counter, firing off pictures from the impromptu photoshoot she'd held with Ted the instant they got home.

"Clare loves him," she announced as her phone pinged.

"Good," Finn responded. "Tell her she can have him."

"Don't be silly. They only have that tiny apartment in the city. Dogs need space to run around in."

"They also need someone who is home with them," Finn pointed out. "I spend half the season out of town."

The skin between Cara's brows wrinkled. "I could look after him when you're gone."

"Your landlord doesn't allow pets."

"I could come here and dog-sit."

Damn, but he liked that. The idea of Cara wandering around his house freely when he wasn't here. Making herself at home. Cooking breakfast in her pyjamas, snuggling with Ted on the couch at night, there to greet him when he got home from a stretch on the road. It felt…cosy. Domesticated.

His heart swelled, warmth spreading through his body. Yeah, he liked that a lot.

"I'm not keeping him, Cara," he said, but the images running through his mind made his tone softer and she smirked at him in a knowing way. He pushed the folder he'd brought in from his car across the counter towards her.

"Stop your scheming and have a look at these." He headed to the fridge and pulled out a bottle of Chardonnay from Cara's favourite winery on Waiheke Island, as she shuffled through the papers.

"You're buying a new car?"

"Not exactly." Finn poured her a glass and set it next to her elbow.

"Then why are you showing me brochures for cars?"

Finn waited until she was looking at him. "I went to a few dealerships after training today before I met you. These are models with the highest security ratings on the market. They have the lowest number of break-ins with the highest-ranked inbuilt security systems."

"And?" Cara said it like a question, raising an eyebrow at him as she sipped her wine.

"Pick one."

She paused, her glass halfway between the counter and her lips.

"Pardon?"

"Pick one."

Cara set her wine down carefully. "For you?"

Finn shook his head. "For you."

"Finn," she said, an edge to her voice. "I can't afford a new car, and if I could, I certainly couldn't afford *this*." She pointed to the figure in large numbers at the bottom of one of the pages.

Finn straightened, folding his arms across his chest. *Here we go.* "I can."

Her eyes flashed brown fire. "You're not buying me a car."

"You need to be safe."

"I *am* safe."

"Cara," he tried to maintain his patience. "You've driven that Toyota since I met you, and it was a shitbucket then. It wasn't even made this century. I've seen you jimmy the door open with a clothes hanger, and now you have a stalker who *knows* that's your car. They can identify it, and they can probably access it if they've got a spare five minutes and a bit of number eight wire."

"I don't care! You're not buying me a car!" She shoved the flyers back to him, glaring daggers. Tension flowed thick between them as he tried to wrangle down his instinct to put her over his shoulder, carry her to the nearest car yard and force her to accept a decent automobile. *Stubborn woman.*

A whimper cut through the air and they both looked at Ted, cowering by his bowls, looking between the two of them.

"Oh, Ted. I'm so sorry. I didn't mean to scare you." Cara slid off her stool and approached the dog, lifting him gently and nuzzling into his fur as she cradled him in her arms. "Daddy's not listening to reason." She glared at Finn over the dog's fur.

He opened his mouth to protest, then closed it again and sighed. "Look," he said, finally. "I don't want to fight with you, but you can't keep driving your car to work. There's a difference between showing that you're not afraid and actively putting yourself at risk. So let's compromise."

"Fine," Cara jutted out her chin. "I'll take public transport."

"Are you out of your mind? That's shutting yourself in closed environments with strangers!"

"Well, what do you suggest, then?"

"We carpool. I can drop you off at work in the morning and drive you home afterwards."

He could see her thinking about it. "What about Tuesdays? We have staff meetings on Tuesdays."

"I'll wait until those are finished." He could go to a cafe or something, read while he waited. Maybe invite himself to Manu's to play video games.

"And on Thursday's I have barre."

"You go to a bar?"

"No, I have barre classes. You know," she prompted. "Like dance meets Pilates meets yoga?"

"What time are those?"

"Six."

He thought about it. "I can come to those too."

Cara scoffed. "I don't really think it's your kind of workout."

"I'm a professional athlete," Finn reminded her. "I'm sure I'll be fine."

"I'll remind you of that when you're sweating like a little bitch next to me," Cara grinned, and he grinned back, pleased to see the last of the anger had drained from her eyes.

"Fine," she sniffed, tossing her braid back. "You can be my chauffeur, but only for now."

Finn nodded. "Thanks for compromising."

She shrugged, burying her face in Ted's fur again so he couldn't see her eyes. "Thanks for caring, I guess."

"Always." He waited a beat, but she didn't look up. "Any chance you're interested in compromising on dinner?"

Her head shot up. "Are you serious? It took us twenty minutes to agree on tacos this morning!"

Finn laughed. "I'm kidding. Drink your wine while I make them for you." He headed to the refrigerator to get the ingredients out. "And tell Ted I'm not his daddy."

"But you will be," Cara singsonged softly behind him.

"Don't worry, Ted," she stage-whispered to the dog. "We're your family now."

~

"How's it going living with Cara?"

Finn grunted and pushed the loaded bar up, settling it into the rack and sitting up.

"Why do you always have to talk to me mid-set?" he complained, reaching for his water bottle.

Manu grinned. "Keeps you on your toes. Stop avoiding the question."

Finn sighed. "It's good. She's good." Of all the people in his life, Manu was the closest to knowing how he felt about Cara. He hadn't admitted it - there was something embarrassing about admitting that you were head over heels for someone who didn't feel the same way - but Manu was deeply intuitive under his sunshine demeanour. It was part of what made him such a great player - he could read people like a book. Finn only hoped he hadn't told Clare.

"No new problems?"

"Not since I started driving her to work." It had been a week of dropping her off and picking her up after work or appointments without incident, and she'd been right about one thing. He was not prepared for barre class. The combination of working smaller muscle groups through the dance positions, aerobic activity and unfamiliar choreography had left him sweaty and exhausted by the end of the class. Cara, on the other hand, had glowed gently beside him, chatting away to the instructor while he chugged water like a lifeline.

"Bet that's putting a plug in your plans, though, right?" Dom puffed up at him from a set of Russian twists on the mat next to the weight machine.

"No-"

"Gotta be hard to take women home with a ch...with Cara already there." Dom corrected himself hastily. One of the other players had imprudently referred to Cara as a 'chick' during Finn's early days on the team and Finn had reamed him out so badly he knew it was something newer players were warned about when they joined. Cara was part of the Knights family, and she deserved the respect offered to all other members. God knows, she'd been there longer than a good number of WAGs, who tended to come and go between splits, trades and retirements.

"I don't take women home," Finn said tightly, lying down and grabbing the barbell above his head.

"Don't want them to know where you live, huh? Smart." Finn gritted his teeth at the admiration in Dom's tone. Their new lock clearly put too much stock in Finn's reputation.

Manu shook his head at the other man. "Don't be an idiot, Dom. He's saying you shouldn't pay attention to what the media says about him."

Dom looked confused. "But he's a legend. Oi, Fearon," he called over to a nearby player. "Chalmers is a legend with the ladies, right?"

Zac Fearon looked across at their small group, blinked once and turned away.

"Friendly fucker," Dom muttered under his breath.

Finn exhaled deeply and lifted the bar off the rack, bringing it in a slow descent down to his chest and hoping the exertion would drown out the sound of Dom's speculation. No such luck.

"An absolute legend." Another voice piped up beside them. Rangi. At least he had an excuse - he was barely twenty-one, an absolute baby. Still a seething mass of hormones, raw talent and financial illiteracy. He'd bought a Lamborghini with his first signing bonus. The woman the team hired to help them manage their money for long-term success almost had a coronary. Dom, though, was at the other end - pushing thirty and still couldn't read the room unless it had pictures. Crash and bash wasn't only his style of on-field play, it extended to his social skills as well.

"My dream is to one day have as many ladies lined up as Charming," Rangi continued, oblivious to the fact his future in sport would be in jeopardy if he didn't stop running his mouth, because Finn would break his kneecaps.

"Fuck off," he huffed out instead between reps.

"Nice language for a potential captain," Rangi snarked. Finn hadn't mentioned his desire for captaincy to anyone, but to players raised in competitive sports environments, the contenders were obvious. A little more leadership in drills, coaches who watched them a few seconds longer. "Hollis has never told me to fuck off."

"Hollis shagged your sister," Manu reminded him.

"Yeah," Rangi sighed. "That was a bit shit."

Finn gritted his teeth and settled the bar again, sitting up.

"If you two spent half the time training as you do discussing my *non-existent* love life," he let the emphasis hang in the air while he glared at them, "maybe we'd be able to start this season in a decent position on the leaderboard."

"Bet you know all the best positions, boss," Rangi sparked up, and beside him, Dom guffawed like a big, dumb yeti.

Rage and frustration quickened Finn's breath, and he glared at them both as he stood and stalked towards the changing rooms. In the mirror, he could see them giving him cheeky salutes as he departed.

Arseholes.

The familiar smell of liniment hit him as he entered the locker room, and he sucked in lungfuls as he stripped. He grabbed his shower kit, knowing he would need to restock after Ted's spa day, but the ringing of his phone gave him pause. Not *Daddy Lessons. Better Man* by Pearl Jam. His mother. Finn hesitated, the urge to ignore it warring with guilt, but it was January, and they both knew why she was calling. He sighed and answered.

"Hi Mum."

"Hello Finnegan." His parents always used his full name. "How are you?"

"Good, thanks." Finn cleared his throat. "And you?"

"Wonderful, wonderful." His mother's tone was light and a lie. She hadn't been wonderful in years, and he was as much to blame for it as his father. That's why their calls were so infrequent, their visits more so, limited to one Sunday dinner a month. Less than that would ruin appearances, and the Chalmers were very concerned about appearances.

Speaking of...

"Your father's birthday is on Sunday, the thirtieth."

"I know, Mum."

"You'll join us for lunch that day?" It wasn't a request. It never was. Still, he'd accept, let the heavy hand of guilt and good manners push him across the threshold once again, despite the fact that he hadn't felt at home in the Chalmers house since he was eleven.

"I'll be there." He paused a second before continuing. "Cara is staying with me at the moment. There's a chance she'll accompany me." Usually he'd feel bad for throwing her under the bus, but since he was pretty sure he was now a permanent dog-owner, she could act as his buffer for one afternoon of glorious food and arctic conversation.

"Lovely," Helena Chalmers' voice softened. "Cara is always welcome."

It might even be true. Certainly she was more likely to be welcome than him, the only child that had shattered his parents' dreams then stomped on them in size twelve rugby boots.

Finn let Helena offer advice about gifts his father might

like for his birthday, both of them ignoring the fact that Finn hadn't bought his father anything but twenty-five year old single malt Macallan for his birthday in almost a decade, until she trailed off. Several stilted minutes of conversation later and he made an excuse about training and hung up, telling himself he imagined the hopeful note in her voice when she said she'd see him at the end of the month.

White-knuckling his shower bag, he grabbed a towel, headed to the stall furthest from the door and cranked the water on at the highest heat. He stepped in, letting hot needles of water pound at his skin. As crappy mornings went, it was a stunner. His reputation had been funny once, an ironic kind of piss-take of the quiet nights he favoured, but it was too big now, big enough that the very mention of it overwhelmed him. Coupled with the silent reminder of his failings talking to his mother inspired, it seemed like simply another reminder that men like him weren't what people wanted. Not the fans, not his family. Not when the lure of the hegemonic fantasy was so tightly woven into New Zealand's very culture.

He hadn't done anything to help himself, he knew that. The underwear campaign and cheeky naked photoshoots had only exacerbated the public's perception of him as rugby league's whore du jour. Not for the first time, he wondered what Cara thought of it. She knew more of his true self than anyone else ever had, yet there were plenty of nights they spent apart. Nights when he could, hypothetically, be boning other people six ways to Sunday. The desire to make sure she knew he wasn't gripped him, but there was no delicate way to bring it up.

Hey, just wanted to be clear that the most sexual action I get is shame-wanking to the picture of us at Piha after graduation.

The heat and steam surrounded him, and the pressure on his sinuses escalated to tell-tale pinpricks behind his eyes.

Shit.

Finn tried not to cry at work. He tried not to cry at all but especially not at work. Today, though, like so many others, tears spilled out, tracking silently down his cheeks to merge with the shower water on his chest. And hot on their heels, shame, flaring bright and hot, coursed through him.

Stop crying. You're pathetic. At this point he couldn't tell if it was his voice or his father's that echoed inside his head. The two had intermingled long ago, and he hated that, hated this side of himself that after all this time still let the ghost of his father's rage and disappointment colour his own feelings, painting them a sickly puce, the same colour as the regurgitated blueberry cheesecake that he'd knelt in while sobs wracked his prepubescent body.

Some people wanted security. Some wanted satisfaction. Finn Chalmers wanted to be loved. Not adored. He had no interest in the fickle rush of hormones that crested and crashed before retreating in thick waves. He could get that from any Knights fan. No, he wanted more. He wanted to be *seen*, to be *known*. To be accepted for his authentic self, his defences and layers stripped away to reveal the pure truth of his soul. He'd been mocked so much as a sensitive young boy that he'd over-corrected in his later years and now the laid-back, shallow costume he'd donned as armour had hardened and set. He could barely peek through the cracks without his team thinking he was joking, and the rest of the country would be no different. The idea that Finn Chalmers - the Prince Charming of rugby league - cried in the shower because nobody loved him would be as fantastical as the possibility of the Knights winning the competition three years ago.

Finn stood under the water until his tears stopped. There was no point waiting until the water ran cold – it never did. The Auckland Knights might not be the most well-funded club in the competition, but no player would put their body on the line for an organisation that couldn't provide hot showers. Finally, he pulled himself together, shut the water off and wrapped himself in his towel. *You're lucky*, he reminded himself firmly. *You're a privileged white male celebrity in a society that celebrates those things. You play a game for a job. You have a nice house, a decent car, food in your fridge and maybe a dog.*

He left one thing off the list he repeated like a mantra as he got dressed and headed home to the very best thing in his life. Even if she didn't know it.

CHAPTER 4

The Pistol Annies blared through Finn's kitchen on Tuesday morning as he descended the stairs, water bottle in hand. Cara, however, was nowhere to be seen, even though it was time for them to leave. Ted lay curled in his bed by the couch, so she hadn't taken him out. The dishwasher drawer was open, rows of shiny, clean plates gleaming in the morning light, the dishes from last night's *Ted Lasso* marathon rinsed and stacked to the side of the sink. Between his training, her work, the late nights she'd been spending uploading the beginning of the year learner profiles online and organising Denise's hen's do, it had been the first chance they'd had to hang out together outside of their daily carpool.

"Cara?" Finn called.

No answer. He picked up Cara's phone, which was discarded on the counter and hit pause on the music. The silence was almost oppressing after the rollicking country beat.

"Cara?" Finn tried again, and this time there was a small groan from the living area.

He rounded the couch and there she was, tucked into a ball, one arm thrown across her eyes.

"Migraine," she murmured, as he lowered himself onto the couch, grazing his hand over her braided hair, still damp from the shower.

"What happened?"

"Can't see. Lost my vision when I bent down to unload the dishwasher."

"Oh, honey." He smoothed his hand over her hair again, and the scent of raspberries wafted up. He sucked it in eagerly.

"Should have seen it coming," she continued with a moan. "The light was so bright and your smoothie cup smelled like shit."

"Is there anything I can do?"

"No. I'm okay." It was such a blatant lie he rolled his eyes.

"You're not okay. You're putting yourself under pressure and you're paying for it." He brushed his hand over her forehead and she leaned into him like a kitten. "You take on too much, Cara. It's not right."

She tried to laugh, but it cracked weakly. "Who else is going to do it if I don't?"

"You are so loved." His words came out too intense, and he hoped her ears were malfunctioning as well as her vision. Or maybe he didn't. Maybe it was better she knew, but not now, not when she was incapacitated. "You have so many people who would drop whatever they were doing to help if you'd just ask."

"It's easier this way," she whispered through dry lips.

"Does this seem easier, Cara? Practically passing out because you're too busy making sure everyone else is taken care of that you forget that you're the one who needs looking after right now?"

"Shhh. No yelling."

"I'm not. Here," Finn said, and pressed his water bottle to her lips. She drank thirstily, and when he got up and fetched painkillers from the cupboard above the refrigerator, she swallowed those down too. He helped her back to her bedroom, easing her onto the mattress and removing her shoes, pulling the curtains to block out as much light as possible before ringing Denise to tell her Cara was unable to make it to work.

He hovered over her for a couple of minutes, but she was already asleep and he was running late. Eventually he bent and pressed a kiss to her cheek, breathing in her scent and silently reassuring himself that she'd be fine, before reluctantly leaving for work.

He might as well not have bothered.

"What do you call that?" Zac Fearon groused beside him as they both watched the ball Finn had just kicked sail into touch a good twenty metres from where it needed to be.

"I call that shit," Finn said. Jesus, his form was off today. He was so distracted worrying about Cara he wouldn't be picked for a school team at this rate.

"Sounds about right," Fearon agreed. "My nephew kicks better than that."

Finn was pretty sure he didn't want to ask, but... "How old is he?"

"Four."

"Right."

"Chalmers!" Harro bellowed from the sidelines. "You're making a dog's breakfast of it out there. Sharpen up!"

Finn nodded tightly. The thing about a coach like Harro was that there wasn't any bullshit. You knew where you stood. Of course, that wasn't always great either.

He rallied for the rest of training, but not enough, and he noticed a few quizzical looks as the team trailed towards the locker room, brushing off Manu's invite to come over for a gaming session and skipped showering. He could shower at home.

Cara was still asleep when he arrived back. At some point during the day she'd stripped off her shorts, shirt and bra, and they lay in a crumpled heap next to the bed where she sprawled in a thin black tank. He let Ted out and fed him, then ordered food and lazed around until it arrived. Ted snuggled on his lap as he watched tennis and did Sudoku until bedtime. He slept like shit, waking three or four times in the night to check on Cara, refill her water glass, tuck the covers back up around her shoulders.

The next day was much the same - he got her to drink a few sips of a vanilla protein shake before she collapsed onto the bed sheets again, exhaustion pulling her eyelids down. Then he attended training, where he stayed for skills and the team run, but eschewed the Wednesday weights session at Knights Stadium in favour of completing his set program in his home gym.

"You okay?" Manu asked when he rang him that evening. "You've been off the last couple of days."

"Cara's sick," Finn said, rolling over on the floor so Ted wasn't able to lick his face. The puppy immediately ran around the top of his head and licked his other cheek. "It's a migraine, but she's barely been conscious the last two days."

Manu let out a low whistle. "Poor thing."

Finn grunted his agreement. "It's happened a couple of times since uni. She takes on too much. This stalker thing on top of it all…" Rage boiled in his gut thinking of it. There hadn't been notes since he'd begun driving her, but Finn wasn't deluded enough to think that meant her harasser had moved on. Cara wasn't that forgettable. He should know. He'd tried to forget her for months after one particular tutorial where she'd boldly and firmly proclaimed that love was a myth used to bind people together in relationships that clearly oppressed women, before he realised it was impossible and let loving her consume him. "It's no wonder her body shut down from stress," he continued, holding out his hand for Ted to nuzzle.

"Speaking of stress…" Manu began, and Finn heard the wince in his mate's voice.

"Shit," he sighed. "Hit me with it."

"Harro was looking for you during the weights session."

Finn groaned. *That's not ideal.* Harro wouldn't give a shit that Finn had done his routine at home. Not when the captaincy was on the line. Not when another *championship* was on the line. Everyone knew that skills won sets, but teams won games, and the Knights were desperate to prove that their grand final win the year before last wasn't a fluke. They couldn't do that without a strong foundation in teamwork. Part of that was suffering together, on the field, in the gym; hell, even in the pub occasionally.

"I'll ring him," Finn said grimly.

"Probably not a bad idea," Manu said. "You need to get that sorted before he sees you tomorrow."

They hung up a couple of minutes later so Manu could join his wife to kick arse at their quiz night, and Finn sat up on the couch out of Ted's reach and dialled Harro's number.

"Hello?" His coach's voice was sharp, but Finn hadn't expected any less. Players ringing after hours was rarely a good sign, and Finn had been lucky enough to avoid doing so until now. The general rule was that you didn't ring Harro, he rang you. Exceptions tended to be for news of arrests or other scandals.

"Coach? It's Finn."

"Chalmers. You're alive then? I wasn't sure, since you skipped training today."

"I did my individual programme at home today. I have the

equipment here, but I should have stayed with the team, sir. I'm sorry."

There was a slight rasp from Harro's end – a hangover from the era when players would smash it out on the field for eighty minutes, then light up a cigarette and shotgun a beer on the sidelines the moment the final whistle sounded.

"It doesn't look good, Chalmers. You're a contender for captaincy, but shit like this makes it look like your head's not in the game. Nobody wants to play for someone who won't give their all, and I won't put someone like that in leadership, no matter how bloody good he is with the ball."

Finn winced. "I know, Coach. I am committed to the team." He paused before spilling his vulnerability into the air. "I want the captaincy more than anything. There's no excuse for my behaviour today."

Another rasp.

"It's not going to happen again?"

"No, Coach."

"Then I'll see you tomorrow. And you'd better be ready. You're going to train like you've never trained before."

Harro hung up without another word, and Finn flopped back onto the couch. He'd got off lightly with the phone call, but there was no doubt he'd be paying for today's transgressions tomorrow. He'd have to set his alarm thirty minutes earlier so he could get a little food in Cara and still be fifteen minutes early to practice. Anything else would look like a giant fuck you to the grace Harro had extended him, and he couldn't risk that, not now he knew for sure the captaincy was within his reach.

He needed to quit waiting for the good things in life to come his way. Time to be proactive - with the team, and with his love life.

~

CARA WOKE in fits and starts, juddering out of sleep, and then pulled quickly back into oblivion several times before she finally forced her eyes to stay open. The first thing she saw was a glass of water on the bedside table, icy condensation pooling on the coaster below. The relief of the droplets against her skin when she picked it up almost took her breath away. She gulped the whole thing down, the heavy darkness that pressed against the inside of her skull retreating with every swallow.

Bliss.

She looked around for more, but the closed curtains and the lump in her bed made it hard to see anything.

The lump in her bed...

She pulled back the thin blanket covering the lump to find Finn, sandy hair mussed, perfect lips open, passed out on his front beside a small wet patch on the pillow. He looked like a Greek god, fresh from the hedonism of Dionysus and the satyrs, if indeed, Greek gods drooled in their sleep.

Poor baby. In the dim light, the lines of exhaustion were shadowed on his face. Finn was so beautiful to look at that sometimes that was all people saw. They didn't look closer. She was guilty of it herself sometimes, of letting that perfect visage blind her. Now that she had the time and opportunity, she studied him in detail. The faint lines around his eyes where they crinkled when he smiled. The full bow of his top lip, too sensual for a man's face but somehow perfect on him. The tiny scar on his chin - not from an injury on the field but from a house party in their uni days when he got wasted on cheap vodka and fell into a Japanese garden. She'd patched him up on the bathroom floor with the tiny first aid kit in her bag - *all the cool girls took first aid kits to parties, right? -* while he stared dreamily up at her and told her how pretty she was and pulled her down for a surprise kiss before passing out on the bathmat. It had taken three of his university teammates to get him into one of the bedrooms.

He's one to talk about pretty. Cara reached over and tugged the blanket back up to his shoulder. Finn had been gorgeous when they met, all broad shoulders and summer-sky blue eyes, his hair shaved as part of a team initiation she found out later, so the stubble glinted like a fallen halo on his skull.

He'd swaggered into their tutorial room and she'd gone mute at the sight of him, desire and embarrassment dual frissons through her blood. He looked like he should be a character in an American teen film - the homecoming king or the hot jock that girls lusted after. And she did lust after him. That was the worst part. She'd spent that first hour feeling like her tongue was too big for her mouth and electricity zapping her every time he spoke. She'd wished she'd worn her contacts instead of her giant tortoiseshell glasses. Thank goodness for their tutor, Richard, who gave her someone else to focus on.

By the end of the session, she'd been able to make eye contact with Finn, to bid him goodbye as they left together. The next week she'd put in her contacts and glossed her lips despite half-convincing herself he wouldn't be there. Nobody showed up to eight am tutorials twice in a row, not if they were optional. But he *was* there. He was there every week. He started seeking her out during lectures and sitting next to her, asking her opinions about theories on child development and educational pedagogy, and by the time exams rolled around they were study partners.

They'd stayed that way for the next two years, in every class they took together. By the end of the first semester, their friendship was solid, and she'd gone back to her glasses and bare lips and a single, manageable jolt of endorphins every time he hugged her. That was still there if she was being honest with herself, but she knew Finn now, knew how friendly he was. He was a toucher, a hugger; at least with her. It wasn't his fault he was beautiful on top of it and she'd learnt long ago not to read anything into it.

Love was a myth, a fantasy.

She'd known that from a young age. Letting herself get carried away by assigning meaning to platonic hugs and a drunken kiss he hadn't seemed to remember the next day would be a mistake on her part. Finn might not be quite the Casanova the press accused him of, but he'd never suffered a shortage of women eager to date him, and Cara had no desire to transition from best buddy to fuck buddy. Hell, if he ever found out about the crush she'd had on him in those early days the mortification would probably send her to an early grave.

She ran her finger across the tiny scar anyway.

Finn snuffled and cracked an eye open. "Whatcha doing?"

Cara smiled softly. "Thinking about the night you got this," she whispered. "Go back to sleep."

He shut his eye again. "You took care of me then."

"Yeah."

"Why won't you let me take care of you? All I want is to make you happy, all the time. You never let me." His words were slurred, weary.

Her heart stopped for the space of a beat, then started again, louder, his words hanging in the silent dark between them.

"Finn…"

"You're amazing," he mumbled into the pillow.

"You're amazing too." She reached over and brushed a floppy, dark blond curl off his forehead. "You're my best friend."

His breath hitched, and a knot appeared between his brows. He opened his mouth, but she pressed her finger to his lips gently. "Get some rest."

She waited until his forehead smoothed out, until his breathing was deep and even again before tiptoeing out of the room.

She'd woken enough as the pain ebbed and flowed to know that at least a day had passed. Scanning the kitchen counter, she spotted her phone charging next to a potted fern and checked the time. Five o'clock in the evening - on Thursday. The migraine had struck her Tuesday morning. She'd been out for almost sixty hours. Wow. That hadn't happened since she was fourteen and reeling from the first big shock of her young life. She checked Ted's bowls, but they were full of water and fancy offcuts from the butcher - Finn might proclaim he wasn't interested in having a dog, but Ted certainly didn't go without luxuries in his house. The dog would eat generic canned food at her place.

Ted's lead was on the counter too, instead of tucked away in the drawer of the entranceway table where she'd stashed it. Finn must have walked him as well. *And he still says he doesn't want him. What a liar.*

She opened the refrigerator. Stacks of individual meals bearing the label of a gourmet food delivery company greeted her. A Post-it, limp from the damp interior, was stuck to a tower of them - *For Cara*, it read in Finn's tidy handwriting. And next to them, a pile of products from her favourite North Otago cheesemaker. He'd filled her reusable water bottle and placed it on the shelf in the door.

What a sweetheart.

"Hey." Finn's voice was soft behind her, and when she turned, he was all sleepy and delicious, the blanket from her bed wrapped around his shoulders. Her stomach fluttered, and she crossed an arm over her waist, willing her nervous system to calm down.

"You're supposed to be resting," she chided gently, pulling

his own enormous water bottle from the fridge with her free hand and delivering it to him.

"Mmm," he hummed. "Couldn't sleep once you left." He pressed a kiss on her forehead. "Are you hungry?"

"Yeah." That must be what this feeling was, she decided. Hunger. For food. Obviously.

"Sit down," Cara instructed. "I'll get you something." She headed back towards the open refrigerator. It was a little early for dinner, but what the hell? She clearly needed to get something in her stomach as soon as possible before it rebelled entirely.

She found two meals of salmon on beds of new potatoes and green beans and pulled them out, setting the oven to preheat. She spun slowly back towards Finn, only to catch him pulling his gaze up from her behind. A tingle started low in her belly.

"Are you okay?" Maybe he was still a little loopy from sleep. Unlike her, Finn wasn't a big daytime napper. If he'd fallen asleep next to her, it was probably because he was exhausted.

"I'm excellent," he answered solemnly, and an unexpected rush of heat slammed into her. *He would be.*

"What are you going to do now?"

"I'm waiting for dinner." He didn't take his eyes off her, didn't change his tone. There was no injection of the light, easy charm he used when they normally spoke.

"Are you going to sit there while you wait?"

"Yes." His gaze roamed across her body before settling on her face, and the intensity of it stunned her. It seemed so at odds with his floppy bedhead, the soft pout of his mouth. Made him look sharper, more dangerous than any man wrapped in a fuzzy blanket should. "I'm good at waiting for what I want."

He could mean anything. He could mean anything.

"It might not be worth the wait."

Finn's eyes darkened. "It is."

"Oh." She wasn't sure what was happening, but she was positive they weren't talking about the salmon.

"I was worried about you," he said, suddenly. "With the migraine. You scared me."

"I didn't mean to." Cara cleared her throat. "Thank you for taking care of me."

Something passed across his face. "I want to take care of you. I want you to rely on me."

Her throat tightened, and it had nothing to do with the horniness swirling in her lower abdomen. "I don't like relying on people."

"I want you to rely on me," Finn repeated.

"Because we're friends?" She could hear the weak plea in her voice. *Tell me we're friends. Tell me you're not turning my world upside down.*

He shook his head slowly. "Because I'm done waiting."

She almost hyperventilated.

"Cara?" Finn stood, the blanket sliding off his shoulders, exposing the contours of his chest, his arms, his abdomen. She'd seen it all before of course, but not like this, not in his kitchen while he gave her sex eyes and she struggled to pull the thick air into her lungs and what if this was some kind of migraine-induced fever dream?

"Yes?" She squeezed the word out and he stepped around the counter.

"Come here."

She closed the distance between them, three feet, maybe less. She was close enough for the heat of his skin to reach her own, to see the ring of darker blue around his irises and notice how he pressed his lips together, inhaling sharply through his nose when a strand of her hair swung forward and brushed his arm. She reached to tuck it behind her ear, but he stopped her, holding her wrist lightly.

"You scared me." He repeated his words from earlier, only now they were gentle, earnest, wrapping about her like a hug.

"I'm sorry," she whispered, staring at their hands.

"Don't be sorry, honey." Slowly, as if he was afraid of spooking her, Finn guided her hand to his chest and laid it over his heart, holding it there as the throb of life pulsed under his warm skin. Her fingers flexed involuntarily, pressing to the taut muscle of his chest for a moment. "I get nervous at the thought of anything happening to you."

"Finn?" Cara whispered.

"Yeah?"

"What *is* happening?"

He breathed out slowly. Then his other hand was under her chin, tipping her face until their eyes met.

"What do you want to happen?"

She knew what her hormones wanted to happen. They wanted her to wrap herself around Finn and climb him like a tree and not come down again until he was so thoroughly shaken that not a single leaf remained, until all he had was spent on her.

But her brain? Her brain, that had kept her safe from her mother's fate so far, was screaming at her to protect herself. To take back the bricks Finn had smashed through, both here now and earlier in their friendship, and rebuild them into a wall around her heart that would keep him out. It was ridiculous, of course. He was her best friend. But that was it, he was closer to her than anyone. He knew all her weak spots. Nobody else - *nobody* - could cause her damage like Finn Chalmers could, if she wasn't careful about it.

"I'm not sure," she managed, and he nodded, the intensity retreating from his gaze. He dropped his hand from hers and stepped back. The air was cool against her palm after the heat of his body.

"I didn't mean…you don't have to-" She stumbled over the words as he turned away, his beautiful face expressionless.

"Yes, I do, Cara," Finn responded. "If you're not sure, then I do." He shot her a look over the rounded muscle of his shoulder. "I've waited too long for you not to be sure." With that, he walked into the living area. A second later the television clicked on. And Cara stood, stunned, in the middle of the kitchen, with his words ringing in her ears.

I've waited too long.

CHAPTER 5

Finn might not be a stranger to sexual frustration, but he sure as shit didn't like it. It didn't help that underneath the constant buzz of desire was a thread of uncertainty. It had been risky for him to tell Cara he'd been waiting for her. When he got back from his morning run she was gone, leaving only a note on the counter telling him Denise had picked her up for a breakfast meeting to catch her up on the last few days she'd missed at work.

Since Finn knew Cara and Denise's breakfast meetings usually consisted of wedding planning and complaining about Magda while they overindulged on waffles, he wasn't particularly worried. Cara would need time to think about the events of last night anyway. She was notoriously indecisive, which was one of the reasons he sent her the online menus for any new restaurant they tried at least three days out. Otherwise, she'd go back and forth over various options for eons when it came time to order, stressing herself out and frustrating even the most gregarious server.

That didn't stop the anxious hum in his blood. What if he'd overstepped? What if she was horrified? Worse, what if she thought of him as some kind of creep, with an ulterior motive all along? The thought niggled at him all day, until he pulled up outside Cara's work and she threw herself into the car as though the hounds of hell were on her heels.

"You seem eager, even for a Friday," Finn offered, and her mouth tightened.

She fished a note out of her bag and handed it to him. His stomach dropped at the familiar thick stationery and he gritted his teeth as he opened it.

It's nice to see you back.

"Motherfucker!" Finn exploded, and Cara grimaced.

"That about sums it up."

"Have you called the cops?" He checked his rearview mirror as he pulled out onto the quiet suburban street.

"Yup."

"Were they any use?"

"Nope."

He gripped the steering wheel until his knuckles whitened. "When did you get it?"

"It came in with the rest of the mail when Denise cleared it. Obviously, they stuck it in there after seeing me walk in."

"You think it's one of the neighbours?" The preschool Cara worked at was in the middle of a leafy suburban street surrounded by residential houses.

"Who knows?" She slumped back against the headrest, closing her eyes with a sigh. "Honestly? It could be anyone. A neighbour. A parent. One of the guys working on the renovation across the road. Or some weirdo who saw me one day, maybe followed me back to work from a lunchtime run to the dairy around the corner for an ice cream. I've no idea. That's what makes it so scary." A tear escaped the corner of her eye and Finn caught it with his thumb before it could track further down her cheek. His heart ached seeing her like this, exhaustion bracketing her mouth, dark shadows painting the delicate skin under her eyes.

"Oh, honey," he murmured, and she shook her head, dislodging his thumb.

"I'm sorry. I'm fine. Can we please go?"

Finn started to protest, but she opened her eyes and stared out the window and he closed his mouth. As much as it maddened him, as much as electricity prickled under his skin, itching to fight her demons for her, it wasn't his battle and he didn't have nearly enough knowledge to find the person hurting her. All Finn could do was take care of Cara and hope the police managed to track this arsehole down quickly. He slipped the car into gear, and pulled away from the curb.

"Let's talk about something nice," Cara said as he merged onto the Northern Motorway. "What do you want to do for your birthday this year?"

Finn cut a glance over to her. "My birthday isn't until March."

"Precisely," Cara said, her red eyes the only sign she'd been crying. God, had she always been so good at locking down her emotions? Had he only ever seen what she wanted him to? "Plenty of time for planning."

Finn smiled, humouring her. "What would *you* like to plan for my birthday?"

"Hmmm." Cara flicked through the screens on her phone. "It's a Monday. That's a bit of a useless day for a birthday. Especially a twenty-fifth birthday."

"What did we do for your twenty-fifth?"

"Wine tasting on Waiheke Island, then the Sydney Smoke exhibition game. That was good for my birthday cos it's still pretty cold in October, but you're right at the end of summer. We should do something fun and outdoors. Skydiving?"

Finn barked out a laugh. "I think the Knights would have something to say about that if I checked my contract."

"Bungy jumping? White water rafting?"

"Christ, no. You realise if my birthday's on a Monday, I'll still be recovering from Saturday night's game? We'll probably end up having dinner somewhere and I'll go home and ice my bruises."

"Poor old man."

"Yeah?" Finn grinned at her and was pleased to see her smile back. "What are the cool kids planning for their twenty-eighth birthdays?"

Cara sniffed. "That's in October. I haven't thought about it yet."

"But if you did think about it?"

"Probably going out for dinner and then home to scarf ice cream."

He cracked up.

"Ooh, I've got it," Cara said. "Hot-air ballooning. You don't have to do anything, just stand in a basket. Zero risk of injury."

"Do you know how many people die each year in hot air ballooning accidents?" Finn protested, and Cara grinned at him, took a deep breath and began belting out the chorus of Tim McGraw's *Live Like You Were Dying*.

He let her get through the chorus but held a hand up when she moved onto a verse.

"Okay, okay. Horse trekking."

"Pardon?"

"I want to do horse trekking for my birthday. You, me, a couple of horses and a gourmet picnic lunch. We'll do it on the Sunday. How does that sound?"

She peered at him suspiciously. "Are you only saying this because you know I miss my farm girl roots sometimes?"

"No." *Not entirely. I also enjoy looking at your arse in tight jeans.*

"Hmmm." Cara pursed her lips but he could see her thinking out of the corner of his eye. "Okay. I can arrange that."

"Organise it and send me the details so I can pay for it."

"Absolutely not. It's your birthday."

"And this is what I want to do, so I should pay for it."

"Not happening, Chalmers. It's my gift to you." Her attention was back on her phone, and he could see pictures of horses on the screen. He decided to push his luck as he pulled into his driveway and hit the button for the security gate.

"It bothers me that you never let me pay for anything."

The look she gave him could have frozen fresh horse poop. "Does it hurt your big, manly feelings that a woman doesn't care about your money, Finnegan?" Sarcasm dripped from each word. He ignored it.

"No, it bothers me that my best friend, regardless of gender, doesn't let me treat them to literally anything, despite me making significantly more money than they do."

"I don't need your money."

"I know you don't." He pulled into the garage. "It's got nothing to do with need. I want to treat you to dinner sometimes. I want to pay for things we're both going to do and enjoy. It makes me feel good to pay for things for people I care about."

"Good for you. It makes me feel like shit to have someone else pay for things for me."

"How come?"

"I don't like to talk about it."

"Cara." He waited until she was looking at him. "It's me. This is becoming an issue for us. I want to understand why."

Cara glared at him as they exited the car and headed

inside. "I'll tell you, but you have to promise to stop bugging me about it if I do, okay?"

Finn hesitated. "I promise to consider no longer bugging you about it."

"Close enough, I guess." Cara headed for the refrigerator and pulled out her bottle of chardonnay. "Want one?"

"No, thanks." He scooped up Ted, who came careening into the kitchen in a scrabble of gangly legs and scraping nails, and waited while Cara poured herself a glass before following her to the living room where they assumed their usual positions on the couch, Ted snuggling on his lap.

"So, my parents," Cara began, and took a sip of her wine.

"Steve and Linda." Five years of friendship meant Finn was well-acquainted with Cara's family. He'd been present at birthday celebrations, graduations, even Christmases on their Taranaki farm with her parents and younger sister Izzy. In many ways, the warm, hard-working Holts felt more like family than his own.

"Right. Well, Steve cheats on Linda."

"What?" Finn sat straight up, dislodging Ted, who whined in protest. "Since when?"

"Since I was fourteen."

"What the hell?" Finn blinked, trying to put it together, trying to shoehorn this information into his memories of Cara's family, layer it over the image of everyone gathered around a table groaning with food while laughter echoed in the air. He loved Linda - she'd welcomed him into her home the first time she met him and had fuelled his fantasies of ideal motherhood ever since. She wore aprons and adopted orphaned lambs and made bread from scratch. Her caramel scrolls were legendary. To think of Steve disrespecting her boiled his blood. "How long have you known?"

Cara looked at him and sipped her wine.

"Since you were *fourteen?*" Finn was incredulous. "Does she *know?*"

"No."

"Why the hell *not?*" Cara had morals, strong ones. She'd made no secret of her hatred of infidelity over the years, whether it applied to Hollywood couples, his teammates, her workmates or friends.

"I caught Dad with a woman from the neighbouring farm in the stables when I was home sick from school one day. It was horrifying, obviously, and I cursed the hell out of them both. I went straight back inside and waited in my room for Mum to come home, but Dad came to find me. He informed me if I told Mum what I'd seen, they would divorce. That he would take the land - *her* land, the land her family had owned for generations - and she'd be left with nothing. She hadn't worked since Izzy was born. From an employment perspective, she had very few skills. He promised me he would never do it again if I kept quiet. He made it sound like not telling Mum was protecting her - saving her and us kids from losing the farm and living in a shitty rental in town on welfare and child support."

Finn swallowed. "You didn't tell her anyway?"

Cara grimaced and shook her head. "That farm was everything she had, and it was hers. Dad handled the finances, all the business side of things. He ran the entire farm and had done so for years. She might have got a payout, but he was right. There's no way she'd retain it in a divorce. She relied on him for grocery money, for God's sake. He would have ruined her."

"So you kept quiet."

Cara nodded, her cheeks flushed. "I'm so fucking ashamed, but I did. I tried to make it up to her in other ways - helping as much as I could around the house, anything I could to make her life easier. I gave up hockey so I could watch Izzy in the afternoons and take the pressure off there. But I still feel so guilty about it. That's why I hardly go home, and why I'm so determined to have my own money, my own independence. I didn't take a cent from my dad after that day. Not for my school ball, not for uni. I saved everything I made babysitting for three years to buy my car." She paused, swallowing hard. "That's why I can't let you pay for things even when you're happy to. I *need* to do it myself."

"And love?" Finn asked, his breath in his throat. "Is that why you don't believe in love?"

She looked at him then, raising her dark gaze from the couch fabric and meeting his eyes. Despite what she'd told him, despite the guilt in her gaze, he felt everything slot into place when their eyes met.

"Yes," she whispered, and his heart ached for her - for the Cara on his couch and the fourteen-year-old Cara who'd been manipulated into keeping a weak, pathetic man's secrets for half her lifetime.

"It doesn't have to be like that," he told her, scooching forward and cupping her face in his hands. Her skin felt like damp silk and he inwardly cursed her father for the damage he'd caused.

Cara smiled weakly. "But it might be. And who, with a lick of sense, would take that chance?"

"I would," Finn said, his mouth mere inches from hers. He leaned forward and pressed his forehead against hers. Her soft, wine-scented breath puffed against his lips and he drew it in as if it was the kiss of life. He gazed into her rich brown eyes, taking note when they dropped to his mouth. "I'd take a chance on you, Cara."

The tension grew, thick and heavy, pressing in on them as they sat like that, with his heart splayed open before her.

"Finn," she breathed, her eyes coming up to meet his, and

the moment grew, stretched, wrenching his heart tighter in his chest with every second that passed.

Then, as he was about to pull away, to retreat with a joke and a smile, pretend this had never happened, Cara tilted her head, and kissed him.

~

So soft.

That was her first thought - Finn's lips were so soft. Cara brushed her lips over them again, then a third time while he sat stone still beside her. Unsure, she pulled back slightly, but he moved forward, those perfect lips chasing hers, both his hands cupping her head as he returned her kiss. Slow, tender, thorough kisses sending waves of warmth rolling through her, as an unfamiliar buzz began low in her abdomen. Cara was twenty-seven years old and had spent six years at the country's largest university. She was no kissing novice. She'd kissed many people - men, women, nonbinary. Hot kisses, hasty kisses, friendly kisses; kisses where teeth clashed and lips were bitten and a couple of truly unfortunate instances where the person she kissed appeared to have taken instruction on tongue motion from the spin cycle of a washing machine.

She could say with absolute certainty no one had ever kissed her quite like this.

Finn kissed like it was his reason for being. Like he'd trained his whole life for this one moment, like it was his World Cup, his Olympic final and his last day on Earth, all rolled into one. *Give the man a gold medal,* Cara thought in the fuzzy recesses of her mind, and then he bit her bottom lip. He held it between his teeth and tugged gently, and she couldn't think at all past the sensations. He tasted like spearmint and heaven, and she was dizzy from it. White hot electricity skated across her skin, over her arms and down the back of her legs. She opened her mouth to him, a small moan escaping as he burrowed his hands into her hair and tipped her chin up, changing the angle, and she saw stars behind her closed lids. Her tongue danced out to lick softly into his mouth and he groaned, a wretched sound, sucking it into his mouth.

He gave her his breath in return and Cara's core pulsed, desire skittering through her to coil low and dark inside. But this was no ordinary desire. Not a trickle, but a wave, catching her when she felt like she might fall, holding her safe as she floated, rising towards the sky on the crest. Attraction, of course, but safety too. Her stomach swooped, and she edged forward, bringing a hand up to clutch at his bicep and it was so big and warm she let her fingers trail under the sleeve of his polo shirt to grip his upper arm. This wasn't just making out. Finn Chalmers was cherishing her. Claiming her. One hot open-mouthed kiss at a time. Intent drove one of his big hands to her hip to yank her forward and she let him; let him draw her further into him, into this flame of desire licking at her, consuming her whole, and *speaking of licking, is he licking my chin?*

Cara pulled back a tiny bit and Ted took advantage to move up even further between them and bathe her cheek with doggy kisses.

"Oh my gosh, Ted, stop," Cara breathed, removing his squirming body from where he squished himself between her and Finn's chests, as Finn slowly untangled his fingers from her hair. "Way to ruin the mood, little guy."

Ted woofed happily at her, then leapt off the sofa and trotted to the enormous pet bed Finn had set up in the corner of the living room. Of course he did. *He* didn't feel like he'd been hit by a lust-bus going a hundred miles an hour. *His* best friend hadn't turned out to be the best kiss of his life, sweet and dirty in all the best ways. Gathering her courage, Cara spun to face Finn, only to find him watching her intensely.

"Well." She tried to sound as chirpy as was possible with tingling lips and her pulse racing like a prizewinning thoroughbred. "That was something new for us."

He didn't answer, but leant towards her again. This time, though, she held up a hand, pressing it against his chest to keep some distance between them.

"Finn, I-" Nerves flooded her. "I think we should hit pause for a moment."

He stopped. Heat still poured from him as her hand remained pressed against his chest. His stormy blue eyes searched hers and the heat blazing there was almost enough for her to say fuck it and rip her shirt off. She held her breath, her resolve faltering under the passion she saw reflected in his gaze, but then he blinked and it was gone.

"Okay," he said, and moved back against the cushions on his side of the couch.

His shift left Cara feeling oddly bereft.

"It's only…you're my best friend, Finn."

"I am."

"I don't want to do anything that might risk that friendship."

He stared ahead unblinking, jaw tight. "You don't think it's natural for friendship to develop into something more? That perhaps the best relationships are built on a foundation of friendship?"

Butterflies danced in Cara's throat. "I mean, that's the best case scenario, sure. But come on -" she forced a laugh, "-how often does that happen in real life?"

Finn didn't answer, just kept staring at the wall.

"I mean, what happens when it's over?" Cara continued, a hint of pleading in her voice. "When it crashes and burns and you go back to dating Olympic gymnasts? If we go any further, I couldn't go back to being the pal you talk to about that kind of stuff."

Finn ran a hand through his sandy hair and hissed out a breath. "Cara, you make it sound like I'm out dipping my wick in the qualifying pool every weekend. I've had one girlfriend - one - the whole five years you've known me."

"And she was lovely," Cara hastened to reply. "Truly. I sent her a good luck message for the World Champs last month. But don't you see? Your romantic relationships…they don't last. You never see the women you date again. And I can't lose you from my life. I'd rather be your friend than nothing at all."

"You think I'm single because I can't keep a girlfriend?" Incredulity laced his voice.

"I don't think that! But you haven't. And I haven't either. Let's face it, if two people as great as us can't find love, that must be proof it doesn't truly exist, right?" She aimed for a jokey tone, but Finn didn't laugh. He didn't look at her at all.

He stood up. "I, uh, I forgot I'm meeting Manu in town tonight. He's got a thing he needs help with."

Cara watched him with a sinking heart. "You're sure you have to go?"

"Yeah, he said it's important." Finn still wouldn't meet her eyes. "Do you want me to grab you a takeaway for dinner before I head back to the city?"

"No," Cara replied. "I'll make something here."

Finn nodded shortly. "I'll lock the doors on my way out. Don't open them for anyone, yeah?"

"I won't." She watched him grab a sweater, and goosebumps skated across her skin despite the warm temperature. Normally she'd tease him for his preppy outfit, but the words stuck in her throat as he pocketed his wallet and keys.

Finally, he faced her and smiled, but it didn't reach his

eyes. It was the smile he used for fans and reporters, not the genuine smile he saved for her. "I'll see you later," he said through his fake grin, and she nodded, watching as he made his way out of the living area, the sound of the garage door opening and closing louder than usual in the thick silence that settled around her once he left the room.

CHAPTER 6

The huge oak front door swung open on silent hinges.

"What do you think you're doing?"

Finn visibly jumped. "Jesus!"

Cara glared at him. "Are you sneaking into your own house?"

"I thought you might be asleep."

"You thought I might be, or you hoped I would be?"

He looked over her shoulder without answering, and frustration left her in a gusty exhale. "Finn. I'm not trying to fight. I'm scared."

He looked at her then, his eyes piercing her. "What of?"

"That I've ruined things. That you're mad at me."

He was in front of her in two steps, his powerful arms wrapping around her and dragging her against the broad expanse of his chest. She clutched at him and inhaled deeply, pulling his familiar grass-and-cologne scent deep into her lungs in greedy gulps, hoarding it in case this was the last time she got the chance.

"I'm not mad at you." His gruff voice tickled the strands of her hair and she snuggled deeper into him.

"Promise?"

"I promise."

"Why did you leave then?" It was easier to talk like this, without having to meet his eyes, so she pushed through her embarrassment and fear. "Didn't you like it?"

"No, honey." He was stroking her hair with one hand now and pleasure sparked in her scalp, running in thousands of tiny golden rivulets through her body as his big hand caressed her scalp. "I didn't leave because we kissed. I left because you didn't want to carry on And because when I suggested more, you were sceptical it could work. I'm not an arsehole, Cara. I want you, but I won't push you. Not physically. Not emotionally." His lips brushed against the top of her head. "It just seemed easier for both of us if I left."

Not there, she almost begged as his lips skimmed her hair again. *Lower.*

"What…what if I did want to carry on?"

She'd tried to go to bed after Finn left. God knows she'd tried. She'd had a hot bath, warm milk, listened to white noise - anything to lull her into blessed unconsciousness so she could wake up in the morning and pretend it had all been a dream, but she'd been unable to. Instead, she'd laid in bed, overheated and horribly horny until she'd finally given up, thrown her earphones across the room and headed down-stairs to wait for Finn to come home.

His chest hitched under her cheek, and his voice was tight when he answered. "Well, then I'd wait for you to tell me and we'd consider our next steps."

"Oh." Cara thought for a few seconds. "Finn?"

"Yeah?"

"I want to carry on."

One second she was secure in his perfect embrace, the

next she was upside down over his shoulder as he strode along the short entrance hallway towards the main living area. He took the stairs quickly, her braid trailing down by his feet as Ted yapped and tried jumping to lick her face.

"Finn!" Cara squealed. "Let me down! You said we'd consider our next steps."

"We're going to," his voice floated above her. "We're going to consider them in my bedroom."

He flipped her like a pro wrestler and she landed in the middle of his enormous bed, bouncing once or twice as he crawled up beside her. He fumbled at the wall for a second and the room lit up, the recessed lights in the wooden roof glowing like stars.

"Do we really need them on?" Cara grumbled, throwing an arm over her eyes. "I was hoping for this to be a lights-off thing."

Finn chuckled, low and dark. "*If* we go forward with this tonight-" he stressed the *if*, and it settled the little spiral of anxiety that was winding a slow corkscrew in her chest "-it will most definitely be a lights-on affair."

"Dim lights?"

"Spotlights. Halogen ones. And fireworks."

"Fireworks, aye?" A giggle burst out of her. "Big talk, Finnegan."

He grinned his sweet, cocky grin, and she relaxed. Whatever happened next, this was just Finn.

"So," he said as he captured one of her hands and pressed a kiss against her palm. "Let's consider these next steps of ours. Did you like it when we kissed?"

Heat rose in her cheeks, but she met his sapphire gaze squarely. "Yes."

"Me too," he said softly and her insides melted. "Would you like me to kiss you again?"

"Yes," she breathed again, and then he was there, his

strong frame pressing against her cool cream linen as the light picked out the golden tips of his eyelashes, the pink tinge of his cheeks. They studied each other for a single second before their lips met and Cara closed her eyes against the rush of sensation skittering down her spine as Finn's mouth met hers, slower this time, but surer. Firm and deep, the luxury version of a kiss and then, when her head was spinning, he moaned. Deep and raw, as if kissing her was the ultimate feast and he couldn't get enough of her taste. He licked into her mouth, moving closer and cupping her head to keep their mouths together as he let out another sound of ragged desire and Cara answered in kind.

Finn's other hand skimmed her hip and travelled upward to settle at her waist, and Cara's nipples tightened to hard points.

"More," she gasped into his mouth and he groaned again, burying his face in her neck.

"How much more? How much can I give you, honey?"

"All of it," she cried, arching her neck so he could access more of the sensitive skin there, but he stilled, raising his head to look down at her, his eyes glittering.

"All of it?"

"Please," she begged, and Finn pulled back to look at her, to check in, because of course he did, her best friend who just happened to be the greatest kisser in the known universe.

"Cara…" Finn's voice was ragged. "Be specific." He untangled one of her hands from around his neck and gently bit the sensitive skin on the inside of her wrist. "Be specific," he said again over her tremulous gasp, "and be sure."

A thrill reverberated through Cara, settling as a white hot swirl between her legs. *Fuck*, consent was sexy. Affection rushed through her, stoking her desire higher.

Such a good man.

"I'm sure," she said, taking care to enunciate. "I can't go on like this, Finn. When you walked out, I almost got in the car and drove into the city to find you. The way you make me feel…" She shivered. "I need you. Just once. Just to get this craving out of my system. We can go back to the way it was afterwards."

His eyes darkened, something flashing in their depths, but it was gone in an instant before he lowered his head.

"Just once?" He whispered the question against the column of her throat and she shivered, the tickling sensation laced with a swollen sense of anticipation.

"Just once," she confirmed. *Any more will kill me. I'll be an addict.*

"What if it's too good?" His nose followed her neck down and she heard him inhale.

"It doesn't matter." She was begging now, she knew, desperation soaking her words. "It will have to be, but please, *please*, Finn, don't make me wait."

"Hold on tight then, honey." Finn's mouth skimmed across her collarbone, nudging the strap of her tank top off her shoulder. "If we're only doing this once, we're gonna do it right."

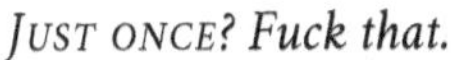

*J*UST ONCE? *Fuck that.*

Finn could barely believe he had her now; Cara in his arms, her soft breath swirling in the air above them, but he knew for damn sure it wouldn't be the last time. *Just once,* she'd said, like he wouldn't burn his goddamn house down for the chance to fuck her nightly. Like she thought he'd be forgettable enough that all the grey sweatpants in the world wouldn't inspire her to give him another go-round. He was a professional athlete for God's sake. He *thrived* on competition, on performing to the highest level. He was going to *ruin* her for anyone else.

"Cara," he murmured, gratified to feel her tense under him. "I'm going to ask you to do something for me."

"Seems presumptuous," she gasped as he wrapped his lips around the tight bud of her nipple through the Knights tank she used as sleepwear. He grinned around the sweet swell of her against his tongue. That mouth. He loved it, the wit it spilled, the way it curved in a smile, the addictive taste of it. He was going to love the way it looked wrapped around his dick too, but not tonight. Tonight was about her, about proving to her that he was the only man she would need for the rest of her days.

"Mmm." He sucked her through the thin fabric, then licked the peak clearly outlined by the damp patch. "Here's what I want you to do, honey. When I do something that feels good, I want you to moan about it. I want to hear how right it feels." He took her lightly between his teeth and tugged. "Can you do that?"

"Yes." She was moaning already, her hips working underneath him.

"Good girl."

Slowly, his hands trembling, he skimmed her top up, leaning down to trail kisses over each inch of her skin as it was exposed. Over the softness of her belly, the smooth skin stretched over her ribs. The base of Finn's spine tingled, lust racing up his vertebrae to settle at the back of his neck, heady and white. His erect dick chafed inside his shorts, tortured at being this close to its mistress. The scent of raspberries filled his mind as he worked the fabric further up her body, the sweetest temptation, and he swiped his tongue up her sternum as her tank top caught on the swell of her breasts.

He lifted the fabric gently and his groan echoed to the

vaulted ceiling at the sight of her breasts, small and perfect, her nipples dark pink from his mouth. She was perfection, a lusty angel, and he would die to find salvation in her pussy.

She worked the top over her head, flinging it God knew where, the motion spilling her hair across his pillows like fire on ice.

Savouring the silken feel of her skin under his fingers, he traced light patterns up the sides of her torso.

"Tickles," Cara murmured, but her eyes drifted shut and she arched slightly, pushing her body closer to him. Her breath hitched as his touch moved closer to her breasts.

Slowly, he dragged one callused fingertip up and over her nipple, circling the bud before brushing across it in a lazy back-and-forth motion.

Cara gasped, and he bent down to swallow it in a kiss, sharing her air as easily as he shared everything else with her.

They stayed like that for minutes, hours, his fingers working her first, followed by his tongue and lips discovering the pressure and patterns that lifted her hips and dragged throaty moans from her. Then his hands were on her thighs, lifting her to meet the slow rock of his hips. Her flesh was soft despite her leanness, a body that spoke of good genetics paired with a good life - cheese and wine and Sunday nights on the couch - and he squeezed it as they moved together, cherishing the feel of her body against his.

"Finn?" Cara gasped above him.

"Yeah, honey?" He didn't stop moving, that slow steady rhythm against the dampness of her cotton underwear giving him life. His dick was so hard it was genuinely painful, but the pain was edged with ecstasy, a silver thread that ran straight to his brain.

For you. She's wet for you. He felt like a fucking god and neither of them had even lost their underwear yet.

"I want to see you."

Well, fuck. That was him told.

He sat back on his heels, and she locked her heels around his back, keeping that sweet, cotton-covered pussy against the front of his shorts as he stripped off his polo shirt. She reached up, spreading her hands across his abs, exploring the terrain of him as he sat there, taking it, letting her have her way. Short nails traced up to his pecs and anticipation wrenched tight in him. She dragged them across his nipples in unison and his cock jerked in his pants, precum oozing down the length of him as every synapse in his brain fired with the combination of it all – the view of Cara topless on her back, her thighs holding him tight against the warmth of her, the sensation as she touched him – curious and bold in equal measure. Perfection. She was perfection.

Then she muttered, "Pants off," and he about lost his mind. She loosened her grip on him and he shuffled back a foot or so to rid himself of the bane of his shorts, his cock springing free in weeping triumph while she worked her own panties off.

He wrapped his hands around his cock and tugged it twice. Firm and quick, the way he did when he was alone, squeezing hard enough for the good kind of white to flash behind his eyelids. Cara made a whining sound, a frustrated kitten noise, and he paused, taking her in. Capturing the moment in his mind's eye before he lost himself to the pyre that awaited. Pale thighs spread wide, a neatly trimmed triangle of red hair at their apex. His gaze followed the lines of her body, from the toned limbs from barre class to the gentle swell of her belly, a glorious reminder of her softness. Her tits, the same ones that had taunted him through long summers in bikinis and plunging necklines on nights out, rose and swelled, tipped with cherry red peaks, and the sight of her spread out on his bed waiting for him, a *gift* for him, was almost enough to undo him.

He leaned forward bracing himself on one hand and with the other he cupped her face, the satin of her cheek filling his palm.

"You're beautiful," he said, and he leaned down to kiss her. It felt like his first kiss all over again, except better. First kisses were steeped in anticipation, in passion, in excitement and he felt all those things when he kissed Cara, but he felt something deeper as well, like a lock tumbling into place in his chest, quiet and heavy and perfect. He pulled back slowly and reached between them. Using one finger, he softly teased her opening, skimming up to her clit in a light caress.

"Ready?" he whispered, and she nodded, whisky-brown eyes bright and steady on him. Finn reached across to his bedside drawer to grab a condom, not missing the way Cara's eyes followed his hands as he rolled it on, her throat working as she swallowed hard.

Concentrate. Make it good for her. Make it the best for her.

He positioned himself at her entrance and stilled. Her petals spread wide around the tip of his sheathed cock, bathing it in warmth. The sweetest, filthiest kiss imaginable. He could come from the sight alone before he was even an inch deep.

"You look so good, honey," he breathed, and she squirmed, working him further into her as he watched.

"More," she sighed, their words light and fleeting now, whispers in church as he sank deeper and they joined together in divine union.

Heaven.

Home.

He kept his eyes on her as he began to move and Cara watched him back solemnly, the glaze of desire not enough to dissipate the earnest gleam in her dark eyes.

"There," she whispered and Finn titled his hips, dragging the head of his cock across the spot inside her that made her breath catch and her nails dig into his biceps. He revelled in it, the tightening of her around him, her fingers on his arm, the vice of her thighs, the clasp of her around his thickness as he worked, building her up, slow and deep and thorough, loving every inch of her inside and out.

Finn pressed his thumb to the soft pillow of her lips and she sucked him inside, laving his skin with her tongue, turning his mind inside out as he thrust slowly into her body and mouth simultaneously. Removing his thumb, he reached down between them and pressed it against her clit, holding it there as they moved together. Not rubbing, but letting the motion of their bodies work the digit against the sensitive nub.

"Holy fuck," Cara gasped, jackknifing up, one arm snaking around his neck and gripping on for dear life. "Holy fuck. It's so good, Finn." She buried her face against his chest and once again the smell of raspberries hit him, mingled with sex and sweat, loosening his hold on his sanity. Around him he felt the telltale quickening of her muscles keeping time with her ragged breaths and he increased his pace, his hips snapping forward like pistons. Cara groaned, low and loose, and he unwrapped her arm from his neck.

"Not like that, honey." He nudged her back against the pillows, his hand going back to its supporting position by her face, this time with his fingers linked through hers. "You're gonna come on my cock and you're going to look me in the face while you do it."

Her head thrashed on the pillow, back and forth, eyes closed. "I can't."

"You can, Cara." He snapped his hips forward again, faster, feeling the tiny tremors starting deep inside her. "Look at me."

"Finn…"

"Look at me, Cara." She was almost there and goddamn, if he didn't come first, it would be a miracle. His balls tightened, the hot pressure at the base of his spine building. He bent down, capturing her lips in a messy kiss, eyes on her so he saw the moment she opened hers, the whisky flash as they fixed on him, and he sank his teeth into her bottom lip. She came, wild and fierce, eyes on his, her pussy clamping around him like a manacle and he'd do it, he'd shackle himself within the confines of her body and her mind and her life because this was nirvana, this was everything.

She kept her gaze on him even as she came down, as her muscles slowly softened around him and the sodden slap of their bodies together painted the air. Then she tightened her fingers around his, a secret signal and he was lost, molten heat flooding his veins as he came, fireworks exploding in his mind's eye. And Cara in the centre of it all, hair spread across his pillow, soft and pliant and *his*.

CHAPTER 7

Cara wasn't having a great day. She'd snuck out of Finn's bed and back to her own room in the wee hours of the morning, but her sleep had been choppy and stilted. By rights, she should have fallen directly into a sex-coma. Barre class once a week had certainly not prepared her for sex with a pro athlete. Her carnal cardio was for shit. It felt like she'd been thrown into a marathon after a few years of happily plodding along in the egg-and-spoon race.

Nevertheless, when the sun rose she'd pulled on a cute outfit and her favourite low heeled ankle boots and bounced down the stairs ready to get back to Being Friends with Finn. And to steal one of his electrolyte drinks. Hydration, that was the key. She bounded into the kitchen with a 'Hey buddy!' and he turned to look at her over the counter, the heat and disappointment in his eyes knocking her for six. He bypassed her directly, his morning smoothie in his takeout cup, and a minute later she heard the car engine start.

She tried to talk to him on their drive into the city, but he put on the Foo Fighters at a truly unreasonable volume and she gave up. He might be mad at her for trying to get their relationship back to the way it had been, but the sexual tension fairly shimmered between them in the car, thick and taut. It was there in the way she watched his hands on the steering wheel as he deftly manoeuvred the car between lanes, his long fingers flexing, the sun glinting on the fine hairs that dusted his hands and trailed up the corded muscles of his forearms. He didn't so much as look at her on the drive, but his bunched jaw and the twitch of his eyes behind his aviator sunglasses betrayed the fact that he knew her eyes were on him. After ten minutes or so, she took pity on him and stared out the window, the tension in the car easing with each passing mile until they turned down the leafy tree-lined street her work was on and he'd pulled to a stop in front of the gate and pushed his sunglasses up onto his still-damp dirty blond hair. She reached for a hug, as always, trying to keep things normal. But the instant she touched Finn, electricity shot up her arms, kick-starting her heart into high gear. Finn's swift intake of breath was audible even above the music and when she looked up.

Well...

His bottomless azure gaze ran across her face, lingered on her lips, naked hunger written across the tanned planes of his face.

Toto, I have a feeling we're not in the friend-zone anymore.

"Cara," he'd said, softly, his nose brushing hers, and she'd almost thrown herself back against the passenger door, fumbling for her bag and diving out of the car with a shouted "See you tonight!" over her shoulder.

"What am I doing?" She mumbled the words under her breath an hour later after her forty-third replay of their aborted hug and Parker, who was currently standing beside her mangling an apple with a child-safe knife, looked up.

"We're making kai, Cara."

"So we are, Parker."

"It's for our friends."

"That's kind of us."

"Except Madison," Parker announced. "She tricked me, so she can't have any apples."

Cara raised an eyebrow. "What happened?" she asked, and Parker launched into a tirade about Madison's claim that Ada had said Madison was her best friend rather than Parker. "But I asked Ada, and she never said that, so Madison is lying!" Truly, the social politics of four-year-old girls was exhausting. Being twenty-seven and stuck in an unexpected sexual quagmire with one's best friend could never compare.

Cara's phone vibrated in her pocket as she was finishing a sit down in the Feelings Corner with all three girls - Madison had indeed lied about where Ada's loyalties lay - and delivering the final line of her speech on honesty.

"Hello?" She waved to the girls as they ran off to play.

"Hey." Desire flared low in her gut. Finn's voice was like toasted marshmallow, smoky and sweet. Too much of it and she'd be a sticky mess.

What the hell. This was the Feelings Corner. She could feel confusing sexy-pants-feelings about her hot-as-fuck best friend if she wanted.

"What's up?" She forced lightness into her tone.

"Harro wants to meet with me this afternoon. Are you okay if I'm late picking you up?"

"I actually have an appointment this afternoon. I meant to tell you earlier, but…"

"Yeah." He sighed into the phone when her voice trailed off. "Where do you want me to pick you up from?"

Cara gave him the address of her salon. "I'll be ready at five."

"What are you getting done?"

She paused for a second before answering honestly. "A wax." A muffled groan sounded across the line. "Are you okay?"

"Yeah," Finn replied, his voice strained. "I got a cramp. How are you getting there?"

"Denise is dropping me off on her way home."

"Good." His voice dropped an octave. "I'll see you then."

Cara's core clenched in on itself. "Sounds good," she managed to squeak out.

She disconnected the call and sat stewing in her feelings a little longer. Finn was perfect in so many ways, but Cara had learnt a long time ago that perfection was an illusion. She had always considered her parents' relationship to be perfect when she was younger, the kind of generous partnership people read about in books or saw in films. Discovering the truth had tainted everything for her, but nothing so much as her faith in love. She'd done everything she could to avoid it since then; dating irregularly, engaging in one-night stands or quick flings when she craved a sexual release. Hell, even her virginity had been lost in a farm paddock, along with her Baby-G watch and a modicum of dignity.

The less time you spent with someone, Cara had reasoned, the less likely you were to actually like them, to be tempted to indulge in brunches, or picnics, or deep meaningful conversations. In fact, outside of Finn, Clare and Denise, Cara's friend group was almost non-existent. She got on with the WAGs and they celebrated and commiserated together when the Knights played, but they didn't grab coffee during the week or go hiking together. Her early crush on Finn had been an anomaly in many ways, but Finn Chalmers was like that, sneaking his way through defences and making a home for himself, whether on the scoreboard or in her life.

That was what made him, made these *feelings,* so dangerous. Cara loved Finn. He was her best friend, and he knew her better than anyone else. If she were to fall in love with anyone, it would be him.

Her Feelings Corner musings sat like rocks in her stomach as the day continued, even as she supervised the climbing wall and helped pack up lunch boxes. An unexpected summer shower fell in the afternoon, and she led the kids in for an indoor dance party while raindrops pattered on the wide wooden porch at the back of the centre.

She was helping Denise set up the craft display for the next morning as Magda supervised the final student pickups when Denise slipped on an unnoticed spill and crashed to the ground.

"Denise!" Cara was by her boss's side in a flash. "Are you alright?"

Denise groaned, clutching at her ankle. "Fuck," she wheezed through her teeth. "It's sprained. I heard it pop on the way down." Holding onto Cara's shoulder, she tried to stand and promptly fell back to the floor, a grey tinge to her dark skin.

"Shit." Cara winced. "Should I get an icepack?"

Denise grimaced. "Yeah. And can you call Jodie and ask her to come get me? I'll head up to the after-hours doctors for strapping and crutches."

Cara grabbed her phone from her pocket and rang Denise's fiancée, explaining the situation as she pulled an ice pack from the freezer and wrapped it in a tea towel. She handed the icy package to Denise as she hung up.

"She'll be here in thirty." Jodie worked for a football club in the neighbouring suburb so the drive wouldn't take too long even with school traffic.

"Thanks, Cara," Denise sighed, working her way up onto

one of the child-sized wooden chairs. Cara pulled out a second one for her to elevate her foot on.

"Sorry about this," Denise said as she repositioned the icepack on her ankle. "Can you ring Finn to see if he's able to drop you off at your appointment instead?"

"He's got a meeting with his coach." Cara shrugged. "I can walk."

"It's raining." Denise looked horrified.

Cara laughed. "It's a twenty-minute walk, Denise. I'll be fine. The fresh air will probably be good for me."

Her boss didn't look convinced. "Can you ring and tell them you'll be a bit late? Jodie won't be too far away. We can drop you off on the way to after-hours."

"No need," Cara answered over her shoulder as she headed into the office. She grabbed her jacket and bag, as well as Denise's belongings and returned to the main room to set them next to her.

"Do you want me to get Magda to stay with you until Jodie arrives?"

"That's okay." Denise fished her phone out of her bag and waggled it in Cara's direction. "I've got some Stranger Things fan theory YouTube to rabbit-hole my way down."

Cara laughed and waved as she headed out, past Magda and the last students on the front porch and through the gate onto the street. She paused there for a minute, closing her eyes and breathing in the thick scent of sun-baked earth and fresh rain as fat droplets plopped onto her upturned face. Summer was great, but Cara preferred winter - the cosiness and comfort of being snuggled up under a blanket with a book, a hot beverage by her side. She and Finn often spent their Sundays that way during the league season, with him nursing various injuries and reading giant non-fiction tomes and her curled up next to him with one of the classics, or a stream of novels about middle-aged women who left their boring suburban lives to run away to someplace like Italy and learnt to make pasta by hand, inevitably finding themselves through participation in village life and some good sexing by a much younger local handyman. This touch of winter - rain in the middle of an otherwise brilliant summer's day - brought those memories flooding in, twisting around her intestines and creeping in to soothe the battered edges of her mind.

"Cara?" A voice interrupted her rainy reverie, and she opened her eyes to see Georgie Shaw's dad peering at her in concern, Georgie clutching his hand.

"Are you alright?" he continued, and Cara smiled.

"I'm great. Just enjoying the weather."

Bernard Shaw looked at her like she was mad. "Right. Do you need a ride somewhere?"

"Oh, no thanks," she assured him. "I've got an appointment up the road in -" she checked her watch. *Shit.* "Well, in about fifteen minutes. I'm about to head off."

"It's raining," Georgie said, echoing Denise, right down to the look of disdain twisting her young face. Cara grinned down at her. Georgie was such a character, blessed with a take-no-prisoners attitude that would win her admirers and antagonists in equal measure as she grew up.

"I don't mind the rain," she told the little girl.

Bernard smiled fondly at his daughter.

"Come on," he said to Cara. "We're parked right here." He gestured at a dark blue SUV parked directly in front of them. "Jump in and I'll drop you where you need to go. Georgie doesn't want her favourite preschool teacher to get a cold."

Georgie nodded. "You're not wearing appropriate wet weather gear," she informed Cara solemnly, a direct quote Cara had made herself this afternoon when the rain started and the kids had tried to pile out in shorts and t-shirts. Her own flowery skirt and shell top offered about as much protection from the elements as the kids' outfits had.

Cara checked her watch again, then relented, climbing into the passenger seat while Bernard buckled Georgie into her car seat, and directed him to the local beauty salon she used. For all of its size, Auckland often operated like a series of small villages, and the preschool staff tried to use businesses local to the suburb when they could. Even Magda brought a bouquet into work each week from the florist on the corner of their street.

She made it with a minute to spare, thanking Bernard profusely and wishing Georgie a good weekend while she clambered out, trying to keep the floaty fabric of her skirt from riding above professional levels.

By the time she was lying on the table, chatting with her aesthetician, Abby, about the other woman's meddling in-laws, she had little to do but think about the upcoming weekend.

Finn's first preseason game was tomorrow against an Australian team who'd travelled across and she was excited to watch him play. The beginning of the season was her favourite part; so much potential for success, limited niggles or injuries, new players, and some new additions to the WAGs box to meet. With the glorious exception of their Grand Championship success two years prior, a season's worth of Knight's games could become almost painful to even watch, tension coiling in on itself as the audience winced at dropped balls and missed tackles. Sympathy and commiserations that were passed through the box knowing that someone's significant other was going to be in a bad mood when the whistle blew and they headed home were rife, the women supporting each other as much as they could. The beginning of the season was more fun - almost a celebration. And Finn, for all that he liked his peace and quiet, was almost child-like in his excitement, fizzing to get out on the field like a five-year-old ready for his first real game.

He was waiting for her when she finished, the Beemer idling outside the small row of shops that housed her salon, and when he looked at her, she could see it there in the ocean blue of his eyes. The anticipation. Her heart swelled as she buckled herself in.

"You look happy."

"Mmm."

"Good meeting?"

He cut a glance at her, grinning, and heat spread under her skirt that had nothing to do with the recent trauma to her hair follicles.

"Harro said I'm shortlisted for captaincy. He's gonna give all of us a run at it during the preseason games, starting tomorrow."

"That's great!" She couldn't hug him while he drove, so she reached across and squeezed his thigh. "You'll be amazing," she assured him.

Finn's eyes lingered where her hand rested on the thick bulge of his quad muscle. "I hope so," he said softly, and she pulled her hand back, suddenly self-conscious about an action she'd never thought twice about. Mind you, they'd never had the ghost of a perfect night riding their shoulders before.

"I want the captaincy badly," he said, sincerity hoarsening his voice. "It…it could change everything for me. Professionally, it's a boon, yes, but the impact it would have on my income, and on sponsorship opportunities, a little more serious than hawking boxer briefs. The profile I could use to give back…" He trailed off, his gaze fixed on the road.

"You give a lot already," Cara reminded him gently. She'd been his plus one at many charity events and he'd never left without making a contribution - the biggest ones always to organisations that supported victims of violent crime and offender rehabilitation.

"A lot isn't always enough," he replied. Silence settled between them until he hit a few buttons on the car's touch-screen and pulled up a playlist titled 'Cara'. She let her head fall back, as the smooth strains of The Chicks 'Wide Open Spaces' began to play, and let the music wash over her as they drove.

Once home, Finn immediately pulled pre-prepared meals from the refrigerator and stuck them in the microwave. She didn't need to ask what they were - he ate gluten-free spaghetti bolognaise the night before every game. Rather, she poured them two large glasses of water, got plates out, and ripped open the bag of salad he'd tossed on the counter. She dished it onto the plates, taking care to scoop any bits of tomato on his plate onto hers instead. Finn hated fresh tomatoes with fervour that was frankly ridiculous and second only to his vitriol towards blueberries.

"How was your day?" Finn asked as he served up the spaghetti with a solid seventy-thirty portion ratio between their plates.

"Good," she said, relaying the argument between Parker and Madison, Denise's injury, the glorious moments in the rain before Georgie and her dad had found her sopping wet and insisted on driving her to her waxing appointment, as she pulled cutlery out of the counter drawer and pushed it to the other side where Finn could transfer it to the dining table.

She was met with a silence so heavy it almost crushed her. When she looked up, he was staring at her, their meals dumped unceremoniously on the dining table, not even in front of chairs.

"You took a ride," he said slowly. "With a stranger. When you're being targeted by a stalker."

"Not a stranger," Cara corrected cautiously. An alarm blared inside her head. *Warning! Warning!* "A parent from preschool. His daughter was in the back seat. And I was running late."

"For your wax?" He crossed the floor in four long strides, eyes focused on her.

"For my *appointment*, yes."

"Your waxing appointment."

"Why are you being like this?"

Finn shut his eyes and exhaled out his nose.

"Show me," he said finally, opening his eyes. She was close enough to see the ring of navy around the ocean blue of his irises.

"Show you what?" Cara breathed.

"Show me," Finn said slowly, carefully, "The part of you that is so important you risked your safety to take care of it. Show me your sweet little bare pussy so that I can see its value for myself."

"Finn..."

"Show me."

It might be phrased as a demand, but his words were soft, lingering in the brief space between their mouths. They brushed across her lips and the tip of her tongue shot out as if to capture the flavour of them. Even as Finn groaned, she knew she could stop this at any moment. He wouldn't be mad. They could head to the living room and sit next to each other on the couch and never speak of it again. If that was what she wanted. Only, she wanted something else. Cara inhaled deeply, breathing in his exhalation, his scent, the sense of safety that was Finn Chalmers, even in this moment with his eyes hot and dangerous, and twisted the fabric of her skirt in her hands. She raised it slowly, inching it up, the sunlight pouring through the window heating every inch of skin she exposed.

"Cara, honey." Finn pulled back and fixed his eyes below her waist. His chest rose and fell in time with her own, harsh and fast, at complete odds with the achingly slow progress of her reveal. "You gonna let me see?" She would have sworn she heard a thread of pleading under the rough question.

"Yes," she whispered, and he fell to his knees, ruching her skirt up to her hips and bracketing it there with his strong hands.

"Oh yeah." Finn's voice travelled up to her. "I would have risked it all for this, too." He pressed a kiss against the front of her underwear, and Cara's head fell back as a shiver skittered through her limbs. Slowly, he gathered the front of her skirt in one hand against her stomach and used it to trap her against the kitchen counter. With the other hand, he ran one finger lightly over the sheer fabric, travelling further each time until he traced her entire slit through the thin barrier of her panties.

"Look at me," he commanded, and she raised her head and looked down at him. His pupils were blown, huge and dark, obscuring all but a hint of his electric blue irises. Keeping his eyes on hers, Finn leaned forward and ran his tongue along the path his fingers had created. Cara shuddered out a gasp and her gaze skated down her body. He hooked a finger into the lace and drew it to one side.

"Beautiful." The word danced across her skin, warm and reverent. His tongue followed, splitting her gently, then more firmly. Cara squirmed, half from the twist of frustrated desire, half from the intimate examination, and he pressed gently on her abdomen.

"Uh-uh, none of that. Stay still while I look at you."

"Finn -" Cara began, her voice high and tight.

"You're so pretty here," he interrupted conversationally. "Did you know that? Prettier than I ever imagined."

"You imag-"

"Keep still for me, yeah? You work so hard taking care of other people. Relax and let me take care of you for once."

"I can't...I mean, I don't know that I can finish like this."

Blue eyes hit her again. "Just enjoy it, okay? Don't worry about getting there. If that's what you want, I'll give you whatever you need. My mouth, my fingers, my cock. Hell, even a toy, if that's your preference, but for now let me make you feel good."

"Okay," she gasped, straining her hips forward, begging silently for him. Finn flashed her a sweet grin and pressed another kiss against the tender skin of her mound.

"Communication, yeah? Tell me what you like." With that, he licked through her folds again, the tip of his tongue brushing against her clit and she jerked.

"Yes. That. Right there."

"Good girl," he mumbled, doing it again, the movement of his mouth against her sensitive flesh heightening her arousal, twisting it tight inside her. Then his tongue settled against her clit, lapping lightly at the sensitive bud while one thick fingertip dipped between her folds, brushing back and forth, breaching deeper with every swipe, until one curl hit a spot that shot lightning through her and she angled sharply at the waist, grabbing handfuls of Finn's soft hair to steady herself as her knees buckled.

"There you are," he whispered, and then he lifted her, laying her on the counter, yanking her underwear down her legs and spreading her wide as he feasted, one arm still banded across her hips, keeping her in place as he worked yet more magic with his fingers and lips and tongue. He'd been exploring at the beginning, learning the shape and taste of her, teasing her with lightness and precision. Now? Now

Finn ate her like she might be his last meal on Earth. Sloppily. Greedily. Perfectly. He growled into her flesh as he tongued her, laving his way up and down her lips, down to where she dripped around the base of his fingers, swirling his tongue around her opening and back up to her clit. He suckled at the tiny bud and Cara cried out, bucking against his mouth, nerves screaming with desire.

"That's it, honey." Finn grated out hotly against the skin of her inner thigh. "That's how it's supposed to feel." He pumped his hand quickly, his fingers lighting a path inside her and returned the flat of his tongue to her clit, dragging it over the sensitive bundle of nerves in slow, thorough, laps.

Pleasure twisted inside her, dark and hot, coiling in on itself, growing thicker each time his fingers stroked that spot high inside her.

"Fuck, Finn," she gasped, and he lifted his passion filled gaze to hers, pinning her with it as he feasted on her like she was a delicacy, pleasure and indulgence in every satisfied hum of his lips, in the way he groaned when she locked his shoulders in place with her calves.

It was his gaze that did it, glazed with desire as he watched her, and he kept it on her as the first tremor hit. He didn't deviate, keeping the same pace, the same rhythm, one broad arm holding her in place as she crested in a rush of white-hot waves, followed by warmth that settled into her bones and weighed her down as the lights retreated from behind her eyes and she sank back against the countertop, loose and messy and glowing.

Slowly, Finn removed his fingers from her and the soft sound of sucking flesh drifted up to her before his tongue settled back between her legs, gently licking the evidence of her climax away. Then he pulled her up, lifting her boneless arms to wrap around his neck, hitching her up with her legs around his waist and she purred as the bulge in his preppy-as-fuck Ralph Lauren shorts brushed against her still-sensitive clit while he walked them towards the couch and she clung to him like a sexually satisfied spider monkey. He deposited her gently on the cushions, fingers flexing on the flesh of her hips, the early evening sun painting him gold, and her head buzzed with the possibility of what was to come.

Except, no. The buzzing wasn't inside her head.

Finn straightened and shot her an apologetic look as he pulled his phone from his pants pocket.

"Shit," he said, glancing at the screen.

"Wha-" Cara gaped at him, but he was already answering it.

"Hello, Finn speaking." God, he'd always had such good manners. She loved that about him. But what kind of manners left her half naked on a couch in the clear light of almost-day while he stepped out onto the patio, phone to his ear? Wasn't there etiquette to these things? He'd gone to a private boys' boarding school for Christ's sake - surely finishing sexual encounters with a degree of elegance made up half their curriculum, along with white-collar crime and institutionalised homophobia.

Cara waited for a long minute, and when he didn't return, stood, shimmied her skirt down and headed for her room, claiming her phone from the counter - *Lord, the counter* - on the way. She didn't bother looking for her underwear.

She closed the door behind her and threw herself onto her bed, hitting the video call icon next to her sister's picture. It rang a few times and then...

"What the fuck, Cara? It's five in the morning." Izzy grumbled, the screen showing a mass of shadows and tangled blonde hair.

"I know." Cara didn't bother apologising. Izzy had rung her at obscene hours of the night for over a decade now, for everything from a ride home, to declaring her sisterly love, to rapping the Fresh Prince theme song for her. "I need to talk to you."

"About what?" Izzy grumped. She was not a morning person.

"I had sex with Finn," Cara whispered.

"Wait, what?" Her screen lit up as Izzy's room flooded with light and her sister sat up in bed.

"What do I do?" Cara hissed. "I'd barely finished and his phone rang. He picked it up and answered it like I wasn't lying half naked on the couch. To be honest, I thought we were heading for home again." The last bit came out extremely bitter.

"Ugh. Too much detail for your little sister," Izzy replied. "My vagina just closed up. And not in a good way."

"You're impossible."

"I'm serious. Fifteen different barriers slammed into place. It's like the opening sequence to *Get Smart*. You couldn't get a hat pin through my cervix right now."

"Stop being cute and listen to me freak out," Cara ordered in her best older-sister voice.

Izzy sighed. "Is it really so much of a surprise, Cara?" she asked. "Finn's been in love with you for years."

Everything in Cara stilled for a moment, the thump of her heart thick and loud in her ears.

"No, he hasn't."

Izzy rolled her eyes, the same shade of whisky brown as Cara's.

"He absolutely has," she said. "Anyone with eyes can see it. The only one who hasn't noticed is you."

Cara was already shaking her head. "You're wrong. We're friends," she protested, sifting through all the times Finn and Izzy had met in her head. There was nothing, no incident, that might have sparked Izzy's imagination into thinking

Finn had romantic feelings for her. "What you think... doesn't make any sense."

"Love rarely does," Izzy responded. "Look, you don't have to believe it, but it's true, and I bet if you ask him, he'll tell you the same thing." Her voice gentled. "Come on, Cara. He might have been harbouring a secret crush for far too long and his aftercare might suck balls, but he's a good guy and he's crazy about you. Be pissy about the phone call all you want but don't use it as an excuse to shut him out now he's finally brave enough to make a move."

"I don't know if I want him making moves," Cara replied, panic building in her throat, and her sister shrugged.

"Were the moves not to your liking?"

"They were. They were great moves, but I don't know if I want moves from anyone outside of a single night."

"Then say that. Regardless of anything else, he's your best friend. You should be honest with him." Izzy's eyes strayed over the screen at the sound of a door opening slowly. "And now you've woken the beast. Hello, Beast."

A little dark-skinned boy popped up on the screen, snuggling into Izzy's shoulder.

"Good morning, Izzy."

"Say hi to Cara," Izzy prompted, and he grinned at the phone.

"Hello, Cara,"

"Hi, Hamid. Izzy was just telling me she'd like to make you pancakes for breakfast this morning."

Hamid cheered and threw his arms around his au pair's neck, while Izzy mouthed a clear *fuck you* over his dark hair. Cara snickered and waved before hanging up so her sister could get on with her day, which now included pancakes. She flopped back onto her bed, Izzy's words drifting in and out of her mind as she turned memories over in her mind, searching for evidence.

Nothing.

Izzy doesn't know what she's talking about, she decided. *She's confusing friendship with romantic love. I'd know if Finn was in love with me.*

Satisfied with her logic, she rolled over and grabbed her latest library book off the bedside table, ignoring the tiny flicker in her chest as she opened it and began to read about the protagonist's first attempt at pasta-making.

CHAPTER 8

Knights' Stadium on game day was a sight to behold. All around Cara supporters streamed in, clad in the team's red and black colour palette, a few yellow and blue outfits identifying the opposition's supporters. Preseason game or no, the loyal supporters who had stuck with the Knights during the turbulent years - and there had been *years* of turbulence for the club - always turned out. The first preseason game every year had an element of hope, a shining light of potential that stretched out in front of all the teams, leading the way to the Grand Final. Trades had been made, injuries had healed, and the sun shone down like a divine light on the emerald green field. Anything could happen.

Cara loved it. She'd been raised on rugby union in Taranaki and hadn't known much about league when she'd met Finn, but five years in, it was by far her favourite code. Even better than the faster plays and harder hits, when the final whistle went at the eighty-minute mark, the game was done. No faffing about with injury time and extended penalties and piecemeal pick and go play. Whoever was ahead on the scoreboard won. And today, more than most, she hoped it was the Knights.

Last night Finn had come to her bedroom to find her. She'd pretended to be getting in the shower, but he'd told her through the door that the phone call that had interrupted them had been Harro calling to tell him he was interim captain for the first game. It was huge - a sign that he was a forerunner for the role in the regular season, and she was as thrilled as she could be for him while her lady parts clenched in empty agony. He'd been a bundle of nerves this morning before he left for the game, unable to sit still, striding around the living area with his headphones on, bopping his head and shaking out his shoulders for over an hour before she convinced him to sit down and eat the energising breakfast she'd made.

"Cara!"

Clare's voice carried above the murmur of the others from the front of the box. Cara made her way over, smiling and waving at women she knew from past seasons as she went. Normally on the first day of preseason she'd seek out the new players' partners and make an effort to welcome them. Today, though, her stomach twisted with nerves for Finn and she wanted to flop in one of the comfy chairs and eat cheese. Fortunately, when she reached Clare, the other woman was already sitting with a full charcuterie board and a bottle of chardonnay with two glasses on the low table in front of her.

"Yes," Cara hissed, throwing herself down and slicing a wedge out of the wheel of Camembert sitting in the middle of cured meats, pates and pickles.

"Help yourself," Clare offered mildly. "I nicked it off the main table for you."

"You're the best," Cara mumbled around her mouthful.

The curvy scientist shrugged. "These games are always better with snacks. How's Finn doing?"

"Nervous," Cara admitted after she swallowed. "He's like a kid on the first day of school today. Buzzed, but restless."

"He'll be great," Clare assured her, and a wave of relief passed through Cara. She believed in Finn, of course, but reassurance from Clare, who was notoriously honest to the point of bluntness, settled her a bit. Hearing that others had the same faith in him to lead the team capably filled her with pride.

"How's Manu doing?"

"Good. He's excited to play under Finn. Interested to see how the new guy goes in the midfield. Dominic something, I think he said his name is."

Cara glanced around the room as she reached for the cheese knife again. "A few new faces here, as well."

"A few missing, too," Clare acknowledged. "I like Lauren. It will feel different if she's not here this year."

Lauren Hollis had been the perfect captain's wife the entire time Cara had been coming to the WAGs box. She supported the team fully, never criticising individual players and was always warm and friendly, even welcoming Clare after the media had written stories suggesting Clare and Matt, Lauren's husband, were romantically involved. Obviously, Lauren had put the blame for the false scandal squarely where it belonged - on her undeserving husband. Not to mention, Clare and Manu's chemistry had been electric to anyone who had ever laid eyes on the two of them.

"It'll be strange," Cara admitted. "I don't think I've ever been here without Lauren."

"She's a badass," Clare agreed, and they clinked glasses in a silent salute to Lauren Hollis.

Half the charcuterie board was gone by the time the players ran out on the field and Cara's heart swelled at the sight of Finn leading the way out on the giant screen above the bar. His picture flashed up, the face of a storybook prince on the body of a man built for sin, his eyes narrow and focused as he sized up the other team. Her heart thunked in her chest, turning over as he addressed his teammates, fanning out into formation on their side of the field. *He's so good at this.*

Unfortunately, that was the last good part of the game for the Knights. The first half was brutal - fast, but sloppy. Filthy play from both sides dominated any moments of brilliance, and each team only had eight points on the board as the initial forty minutes came to a close.

"It's a mess," Clare muttered as they watched the team trail off the field. The screen focused on Finn again, his hair caked with what looked like dried blood, streaks of dirt on his face and arms. He didn't look like a prince now. He looked like a warrior, exhausted from battle. And the game was only halfway through.

Another couple of women joined them on the couches and Cara fetched another bottle of wine as they talked through the first half, both shooting her sympathetic looks. It was like that with sports. The players' partners became an extension of them and it didn't matter that Cara and Finn hadn't been romantically involved until a week ago, they were a package deal. Even now, one of the new women leaned forward and said, "I'm Rosie. You're Finn Chalmers' girlfriend, right?"

"Oh no," Cara replied, laughing breezily, the way she'd practiced in the mirror through high school when she was desperate for Tommy Dorfsen to notice her and completely oblivious to the fact Tommy Dorfsen was busy noticing Grant Lansing. "We're just friends."

"Oh," the new girl smiled. "That's nice that you come and support him."

Cara's spine prickled. "Well, I'm really here for the snacks," she joked, and the others laughed.

A sudden thought hit Cara out of the blue. *What happens when he brings a partner here? When he meets someone he's serious about?* There had been Natalie of course, the lovely Olympic gymnast, but she'd never come to the box. Likely it had clashed with her own training. But the way people talked to Cara in here - the intertwining of her life and Finn's, the way people already saw them as a pair. That was something she'd never had to face head on. It simply was, and the idea someone else might come into this space one day, someone who had a closer connection with Finn in the eyes of the WAGs, the team, the media…it made her skin crawl.

I don't want him to leave me behind. I don't want someone else taking my place.

The thought left her cold, a steel knife against her sense of reality. Like this thought, this selfish and unreasonable notion, could leap forward from her mind and rip through the fabric of her relationship with Finn, stripping her of all pretence, leaving her exposed.

A warm hand touched her arm, calming the goosebumps covering her skin. "Are you okay?" Clare asked.

"Fine," Cara smiled. It was a fake one of course, but for all of Clare's academic genius, she wasn't great at reading people, and she nodded towards the TV.

"Second half is starting."

It was as gruesome to watch as the first had been. The only saving grace for the Knights was that their opposition played as poorly as they did. The one bright moment of potential glory came in the sixtieth minute when Rangi Katu made a huge break down the left-hand side of the field, passing the ball to Finn, who carried it almost to the try line before fumbling it before the white painted touchline.

Groans echoed around the stadium and Cara's heart

ached for Finn as she watched him on the screen, dirty and frustrated, clearly swearing, as he made his way back up the field with his head down, not bothering to acknowledge the shoulder slaps of support from his teammates.

"Rough one," Rosie said, shooting her a glance, and Cara smiled tightly.

"He'll be upset with himself for that," she admitted. No point denying it. "Sorry, I didn't catch who you were here for."

"Oh!" Rosie's face lit up like a Christmas tree. "We met Matt Hollis in a bar last weekend and he invited us to the game today. That's Meredith." She pointed to her friend, who was chatting to Clare. "We thought it was really nice of him."

Cara's smile was granite now. "It was. It's nice to have you here."

Fuck you, Matt Hollis. She was going to spit in his beer the next time she saw him. Rosie and her friend seemed lovely, but inviting two women from a bar to the box only weeks after he and Lauren had split was a dick move if ever there was one. Cara made a mental note to send Lauren a box of her favourite macarons and to send Matt a strip of condoms dipped in habanero juice.

Finally, *finally*, the ordeal was over. The Knights slumped on the ground, defeated while their opponents high-fived around them.

Not that they'd played well either. The scoreboard showed there was only two points difference between the teams.

Cara made her way down the stairs slowly behind the others, but Clare was waiting for her at the bottom.

"Are you coming to the aftermatch function?"

Cara shook her head. "I think I'll wait for Finn here. We might be over later."

"Suit yourselves." Clare shrugged and headed off with the

others to the aftermatch room, where the Knights' management would provide food and drink for both teams and their guests.

Cara leaned against one of the large concrete walls near the changing room and pulled out her phone to check her notifications and flick off a couple of emails about Denise's hen's party. She'd only been there a few minutes when Harro came storming out, his face red.

"Cara," he grunted.

"Brian," she responded. "Tough one today."

"Not a good start," he admitted. Brian Harrington could be a hard-arse of a coach, she knew that, but he never treated the player's significant others with anything less than total respect. "Finn'll have to face up to the media after this since he was captaining today."

"Nothing they can say will be worse than what he's saying to himself," Cara declared, and the coach nodded briskly.

"There's something going on with him at the moment. You got any ideas?"

Cara's gut churned. Finn was only twenty-four, and had never had a serious injury. The only difference in his life this season was the fact that she was living with him. *Am I impacting his playing?*

"Nothing I can think of," she croaked and Harro scowled.

"Let me know if you think of something," he ordered.

"Sure thing."

"Hell of a rough one for him," the grizzled coach sighed. "I needed a little more from him in the captain's position today."

"He can do it," Cara assured him. "You know that. You know how good he is, with the players and the ball. He was a bit off today."

Harro cracked a smile. "You're a good friend sticking up

for him, Cara. Some of the girls won't even look me in the eye and here you are telling me to give him another shot."

Cara grinned back. "Teachers," she joked. "We love telling people what to do."

Harro threw his head back and laughed, the sound bouncing off the high concrete walls, as Finn emerged from the changing room.

"Everything alright?" he asked, and Cara's grin melted from her face as she took him in, six feet of muscle and masculinity in finely woven merino, damp hair curling over his forehead.

Whew, boy. The man could wear the hell out of a suit.

"All good," she managed lightly. "How are you?"

"Been better," he shrugged and she nodded.

"Do you want to go to the aftermatch? We could always sneak away if you'd rather," she suggested and his eyes lit up with mischief that was snuffed out as soon as Harro cleared his throat.

"Better go and do the captain thing." Finn grimaced as he spoke.

"Media first," Harro reminded him and Finn nodded bleakly.

"Meet you there?"

"Of course," Cara replied. "Want me to take your bag?"

"That'd be great." Finn offloaded the mid-sized sports bag onto her shoulder and it swung against her hip. "Get them to put your drink on my tab."

"Maybe just this once," she shot back cheekily, and he smirked indulgently before following Harro towards the media suites.

Cara made her way to the aftermatch function room, dropping Finn's bag in the corner with the others his team-mates had abandoned and got herself a Sprite from the bar, paying for it herself. She didn't feel so sorry for Finn that she'd let him buy her drinks, even if he did know now the reasons behind her insistence on paying her own way.

Clutching her beverage, she made a beeline for Clare's table, only to stop when the room fell silent, all eyes on the screen above the bar. Swivelling on her heel, she saw Finn in his suit next to Harro, lined up behind a bank of microphones and sponsorship paraphernalia. But that wasn't what made the glass slip from her hands and bounce off the plush charcoal carpet.

No, that was the sight of her best friend crying on national television.

~

Fuck.

Heat flushed up Finn's neck and face as he wiped his eyes as discreetly as possible. Not that it did much good with half the country's sports cameras on him. A single tear from each eye, maybe a second from the left one, but that was it. Brought on by a routine question about his dropped pass in the second half. But it was more than that, he knew it, even as he swallowed hard and fixed his eyes on a spot on the back wall. The pressure had built since Harro called, interrupting his couch time with Cara. It had buzzed under his skin, stretching his muscles taut and skimming across his nerve endings, leaving him raw and exposed. He'd ignored it, tried to push it down and wrestle it into submission the way he did with all his uncomfortable feelings. It might not be healthy, he knew that, but it *was* effective. At least until now. When two, maybe three, tears leaked their way out to make him a national laughingstock.

"Charming?" The reporter, JJ something, a tiny blonde with a podcast who'd somehow wrangled her way in with the heavy hitters and who'd asked the question about his dropped pass, spoke again. "Are you okay?"

Beside him, Finn could feel Harro's eyes on him. *Double fuck.* There was no point trying to blame hayfever; he'd rolled around on fresh-cut grass for the last two hours. *I've got to own it.* Harro wouldn't like it, but Harro didn't like much apart from Glenfiddich, cheese rolls, and winning.

"Sorry, JJ." He cleared his throat, trying to swallow away the vestiges of emotion that clung to his windpipe. "It was a tough battle out there, and the first game always brings up a few feelings. I wanted to lead the lads well, but it wasn't my best game. I'm not happy with how I played, and that dropped ball is only part of it." He met the reporter's eyes and was relieved to see compassion there instead of condemnation. "I'll do better next week and I know the team will as well."

Under someone else. There was no doubt in Finn's mind he wouldn't be leading the team out for their next game. This had been his shot, and he'd blown it.

Unfortunately, the other reporters had caught the scent of blood in the water, and they directed the remainder of their questions to Finn, each one sliding further from legitimate questions about the game and more into enquiring about his mindset. He didn't let another tear out, but his head was throbbing by the time Harro called the press conference to a halt.

"Bloody vultures," Harro muttered as they made their way out the door. "You alright, boy?"

"Yup." Finn couldn't bring himself to make eye contact with his coach.

Harro harrumphed. "Don't forget Tom if you need him."

"I won't." Tom Sebastian was the team psychologist. Finn had never had a reason to call him, and he wasn't going to start now.

"Finn!"

There she was. The only person he needed to talk to jogged towards him with his gear bag slung across her shoulder. Cara dropped the bag and threw herself at him as soon as she got within arm's reach and he wrapped his arms around her as tight as possible, as if he could absorb her into his body if he wished it hard enough.

They stood holding each other in silence. At some point Finn heard Harro shuffle off, but he didn't lift his head from Cara's shoulder. She'd started stroking the short hair at the base of his skull, sending glorious sensations skittering down his spine, and it was all he could do not to fall to the ground and beg her to marry him immediately.

Be normal, he warned himself, even as he nuzzled closer and inhaled her scent. They swayed back and forth gently in the wide corridor, an unconscious dance of comfort in the arms of his first love, under the black and red banner of his second. She didn't even seem aware they were moving, but he took every opportunity to press her against him, her hip, her leg, her stomach and breasts, and memorise them. Slowly, the humiliation of the loss and his lapse in stoicism drained from his body, leaving behind only warmth that spread through his limbs and pulsed in time with the heavy thud of his heart.

"How are you doing?"

"Shit," he mumbled.

"I figured. You wanna blow this popsicle stand?"

"Can't." Finn lifted his head but kept his arms right where they belonged around her. "Gotta do the speech."

Cara wrinkled her nose. "We could tell people you got sick."

"I don't need any more talk about my bodily functions."

She smiled sympathetically at him and he let his head drop forward until their foreheads pressed together.

"So much for the captaincy," he sighed.

"They'd be idiots not to give it to you anyway. You're the best they have," Cara lied stoutly to him, and he loved her for it. They knew both Manu and Victor Hewitt had strong enough leadership to make excellent captains.

"Tell Harro that to his face."

"I will."

He huffed out a laugh. *She would too.*

"Don't do it while I'm nearby. I don't want to be caught in that crossfire." He stepped back, linking their hands and swinging lightly as they made their way back along the corridor, bending to scoop up his bag as they went.

The aftermatch room quietened when they walked in. Not full silence. A hum of chatter still echoed around the spacious suite, but definitely a step down from the dull roar that had met them when Finn pulled the door open. His teammates and today's opponents studied him openly, and he caught the tail end of a few smirks as he made eye contact with each one of them.

Fuck them. Let them try to say something. He wasn't ashamed of his passion for the game or anything else.

In the end though, it was Rangi who stepped forward in the quiet. Rangi, with the top button of his shirt undone and his tie askew, who clapped him on the shoulder.

"Want a drink, cap?"

"I wouldn't say no to a beer." He glanced at Cara. "You okay to drive my car home tonight?"

"Of course."

"Right then." Rangi turned towards the bar that ran along one wall of the room. "Someone get the man a beer!"

Zac Fearon was already walking towards them, a pint glass filled with amber liquid in his hand. Since Zac was a known teetotaller, Finn reached out for it with his free hand and Zac passed it to him.

"Tough game, mate," Zac muttered.

One by one, the Knights players swung by the table Finn and Cara positioned themselves at. Some offered condolences, more offered a handshake or backslap. Dom grabbed a platter of canapés off one of the sponsor tables and plonked it in front of Finn, causing Clare to smile at him in approval and Manu to scowl at him and wrap his arm around his usually standoffish wife.

The players were served meals at the long tables that took up half the main room, but Finn stayed with Cara, Clare and a couple of other WAGs in the corner nursing his beer until it was finished. After a quick speech congratulating the other team, thanking the Knights' main sponsors and declaring rugby league the winner on the day, he locked eyes with Cara and tilted his head towards the exit.

He leaned against the leather headrest of the passenger seat as Cara navigated the roads around the stadium, streetlights illuminating patches of Auckland in quick flashes as they drove, Racing playing softly through the speakers. They'd seen the New Zealand band play a few times and the music always took him back to sweaty nights on crowded dance floors with Cara swaying next to him, feeling like a god on the heady combination of music and euphoria that live shows always produced.

I should play music more often. He played it in the car and when working out, but never had it in the background at home. Since Cara moved in, he found he'd enjoyed wandering into the kitchen and being greeted with music. Even more so when the sight of Cara shaking her booty to the beat also greeted him. Her tastes might run a little more country than he'd ever dared admit he liked, but seeing her enthusiasm for it brought a smile to his face every time. Even the tracks where women sang about murdering men who'd done them wrong, and there were a lot of those on her playlists.

"Would you murder me if I cheated on you?"

"Nah." She slid him a sly smile. "I'd never talk to you again though. It'd be a fate worse than death."

He grinned back, relaxed and happy, until the chime of his phone echoed on the car's Bluetooth.

Mum: See you tomorrow for your father's birthday.

His buzz dissipated immediately, an icy chill creeping across his body.

"Who is it?" Cara asked as she turned into the gated community.

"Mum. It's my dad's birthday tomorrow and I have to go to lunch at their place." His reluctance was obvious in his tone and he hesitated, wanting to ask her to come, but a sliver of doubt crept in. He'd spent over a decade trying to keep his worlds as far apart as possible for fear of what would happen when the curtain lifted on the ugliness that hid behind the Chalmers family name and reputation.

"Want some company?" She wasn't even looking at him and she could read what he needed.

"I'd love it," he answered truthfully. "You don't mind?"

"Whatever you need." She parked the car and smiled at him.

"Can I sleep with you tonight? Just sleep," he hurried to add in case she thought he was milking the loss to get a leg over.

Instead, her face softened, a hint of vulnerability creeping into her dark eyes.

"Yeah. I'd like that. Take me to bed, Finnegan."

CHAPTER 9

*I*f Cara thought Finn's house was a tad intimidating, it was nothing compared to the sweeping mausoleum grandeur of his childhood home. Somehow in all their years of friendship, she'd never set foot in Edward and Helena Chalmers' house - always meeting them out for dinner, stilted awkward affairs that left Cara grateful for her own family, as messed up as it was. Beside her, Finn's fingers gripped the steering wheel rhythmically as he stared ahead at the imposing structure, a muscle working in his jaw, and Cara considered that her absence at Chalmers' events until this point was probably not accidental.

She waited a minute or two more, but Finn showed no signs of exiting the car. He'd been quiet all morning, smiling at her over the breakfast he'd cooked and checking she was okay with a gentle hand to her hip every time he passed her as she did the dishes, but any hint of his usual ease was missing. It was as if the loss the night before had changed something in him, contained a part of himself that she'd never seen before.

"I hate this place," he muttered under his breath, and

understanding dawned on Cara like the summer sun. *It's not the game that did this. It's coming here.* It must have weighed on him more than she'd realised.

Reaching across, she covered one of his hands with hers. He linked their fingers and squeezed.

"It'll be okay," she reassured him. "We'll get through this and we'll go home, make some popcorn and watch anything you want."

He slid her a look. "Even *1917?*"

Cara grimaced. *Fucking war films.* "Even *1917,*" she promised. "And I won't even cry."

"Yes, you will."

"Yes, I will," she agreed. "But I'll try to do it silently so you don't notice."

Finn grinned at her suddenly, his genuine smile cracking through the stoic facade he'd shouldered since they woke, fully clothed, wrapped around each other.

"You can cry on my shoulder anytime, Cara."

Her chest constricted. "You too," she replied lightly.

He raised a sardonic brow. "I think everyone's seen enough of my tears for now."

He wasn't wrong. The news media was full of reports of the press conference, photos of Finn wiping at his eyes front and centre. Even the Australian press was covering it. She'd confiscated his phone after finding him scrolling through the comments of one article on his reported weakness. Nothing good ever came from reading the comments.

"Come on, then," she prompted.

"'Once more into the breach,'" he sighed, lifting their joined hands and dropping a kiss on the back of hers.

They exited the car and made their way towards the massive colonial villa in silence. Finn knocked once on the glossy black door before entering.

Dove grey carpet softened their footfalls as he led her by

the hand past a gleaming dark wood staircase and through several rooms steeped in understated elegance then through a wide set of French doors set with stained glass to a patio overlooking a full-sized grass tennis court. The swimming pool gleamed behind it, the entire view painted in the jewel tones of the nouveau riche.

"Holy Serena Williams," Cara muttered under her breath, and he flashed her a quick grin.

"It's a bit much."

"No worries, Finnegan. I always knew you were a boujee bitch."

He chuckled, stopping abruptly when a voice called out in modulated tones.

"There you are, darling!"

Helena Chalmers walked towards them in crisp tennis whites, arms outstretched. Finn's mother was a stunning woman. She had the same blue eyes as her son, though Cara had never seen them sparkle with Finn's natural humour. Her blonde hair was sliding gracefully to grey and cut with military precision, parted to one side, to brush her shoulders, with the majority falling to the left, almost obscuring a barely noticeable thin scar running from cheek to chin. She dressed fabulously, sportswear included apparently, and the only reason Cara hadn't asked before about where she bought her clothes was the bone-deep knowledge she wouldn't be able to afford to set foot in Helena's favourite boutiques.

"It's so lovely to see you, dear." She enveloped Finn in a hug and Cara caught a whiff of Chanel Number 19. Finn bought her a bottle every year for her birthday. Never Number 5. Everyone else wore Number 5, he'd told Cara the first year she'd gone shopping with him, and Helena Chalmers was not like everyone else.

"And Cara, so wonderful to have you here." Then she was

being embraced in Helena's toned arms and the scent of green woods with powdery florals.

"Thank you for inviting me," she managed, and Helena smiled warmly in response.

"It's a joy to have you joining us. Please, take a seat," she motioned to the patio table, set with snowy linen and glistening silver, a low vase of pale pink roses in the middle. "Edward will be with us shortly. He's having a quick shower after our game."

They sat around the table and sipped on champagne that Finn poured for them before he placed the bottle in an ice bucket and filled his own glass with water. Helena asked about Cara's work and gave appropriate tinkling laughs at her anecdotes of the children and their paint-based misadventures before turning to Finn.

"Finnegan, we missed you at the library fundraiser at the beginning of the month."

Cara watched as Finn took an easy sip of water, but Cara noticed his knuckles were white against the glass.

"Sorry, Mum," he responded. "I had a prior commitment. I sent a generous donation, though."

"I should hope so. Libraries are the backbone of society." Helena nodded towards Cara. "Perhaps you can convince my son to come out in public a little more. The cheques are lovely, but it's really his profile that does the best work in raising donations, you know."

"I'm sure it does," Cara murmured, unsure why Finn hadn't attended but incredibly sure the only prior commitments he'd had in the first few weeks of the year were training and escorting her to the movies to watch a rescreening of *The Rocky Horror Picture Show*. She'd brought gluten-free toast for him to throw.

"Leave the boy alone, Helena." Edward Chalmers' voice cut through the air. "If he wants to spend his time throwing a ball around like an overgrown ape instead of giving back to the community, who are we to judge?"

You sound pretty judgy to me, Cara thought, but stayed silent as Finn rose and shook his father's hand.

"Happy birthday," he offered flatly, handing over the wooden box that held three thousand dollars' worth of whisky and absolutely zero sentimental value. Cara had almost vomited when she'd first seen the price, but Finn bought the box every year, shipped from some whisky broker in Scotland.

Edward raised the box slightly in acknowledgement and took a seat. Despite the warm weather, he wore dress pants and a button-down shirt, polished Oxfords on his feet.

"Hello Cara," he said, as Helena jumped up to pour him champagne. "You look lovely."

"Thank you," Cara replied, fighting not to look down at her simple cotton sundress in case he was pulling the piss. "Happy birthday, Mr Chalmers."

"Edward, please." He waved his hand the way he always did when she called him that and she ignored it as she always did. Edward had none of Helena's openness. Every time she'd met Finn's father, she'd felt the encounter was akin to cage-swimming with sharks. Technically safe, but danger lurked deep in the shadows.

"To another year of life and wisdom," Helena trilled, raising her glass. Cara followed suit, Finn's water glass joining the others in the centre of the table a moment later.

The bubbles in her glass were a direct contrast to the staid atmosphere, and Cara's patience for the falsity waned further when Edward discreetly checked his watch.

A statuesque woman in a black cotton shirt and pants arrived shortly after, wheeling a trolley laden with food and Cara barely had time to be delighted by the prospect of a catered lunch before Finn murmured "Thank you, Serena," and understanding almost knocked her onto the porch floor.

Staff? Who in New Zealand has actual staff? She'd always known Finn came from money – and lots of it – but this was a whole other stratosphere. She shoved half a pork belly bao bun in her mouth to keep her jaw from dropping as she mentally ran through the times he'd tagged along on her second-hand clothes shopping trips.

Serena, for all the shock her appearance had caused Cara, was clearly an angel though. The buns were accompanied by tender lamb fillet, Aoraki salmon and dukkah-roasted cauliflower that Serena assured Finn was gluten-free. Several salads and a dish of honey-glazed root vegetables sat amongst the main dishes on the table and Cara revelled in the few minutes of silence after everyone had filled their plates and she could appreciate the delicious food.

Helena was not so easily satisfied.

"That was a disappointing loss last night," she said as Cara forked a rich mouthful of salmon past her lips.

Finn's jaw tightened. "Yup."

"There's always next week," his mother offered.

Edward grunted beside her. "Probably the poor leadership."

Oof, here we go. Part of Cara had wondered why Finn had asked her to attend his father's birthday this year, but right now, in this instant, she knew exactly why. *What a cockhead.*

"You'd be braver than me to criticise Brian Harrington's leadership after the career he's had." Cara kept her voice purposefully light.

"Well, Harrington's a decent fellow for a footy player of course," Edward grumbled, and Cara stared at him, incredulous at the disclaimer. "But there's not a lot he can do from the coach's box. Strong on-field leadership is what the

Knights need if they're ever going to be in the running for another championship."

Finn stared at the tennis court, jaw tight, eyes hollow.

"It's only preseason," Cara pointed out. She pushed some cauliflower around her plate but didn't lift any to her mouth. She needed her mouth empty if this was going to kick off properly. Besides, she couldn't risk having her knife in use in case the desire to stab her host in the thigh overcame her.

"It's an indicator," Edward argued.

"It's an indicator the team is building momentum. All the other franchises are in the same position at this time of year."

Edward smiled at her through his teeth. "None of the other teams have a player weeping on television like a little girl."

Oh, you enormous bastard.

"Little girls tend to be some of the strongest and most resilient people I've ever encountered." Cara shrugged, the pretence of civil conversation waning. "They're also the most vicious. As a comparison, you could hardly make a less salient point. One of the most pressing problems we face as a nation is the idea that a man showing emotions is a weakness."

"Hardly," Edward snorted.

"Leave it, Cara," Finn muttered. "It's not worth it."

"Well, except anger perhaps." Cara ignored Finn to let her glance flick dismissively across Edward, and his jaw clenched as he clocked it. "Rebranding anger as the only acceptable masculine emotion explains why so many of our men are stunted emotionally."

"Is that what you think, boy?" Edward nodded at Finn, derision flooding his features. "You think being a national laughingstock is something to be proud of? You think your mother and I should hold our heads up high because our son blubbers on TV like a little pussy?"

Finn's eyes slid to his father's. "You haven't been proud of me since I was eleven," he responded evenly. "I doubt anything I do now will make a difference."

Beside her husband, Helena wrung her hands.

"I don't think we should talk about this-" she began, her voice tremulous, but Edward cut her off.

"We should talk about this." Edward slammed his hand on the table, and the silverware jumped. "You could have been anything. We gave you every opportunity," he directed at Finn. "You threw it all away to be a fucking footballer with a bullshit teaching degree," he sneered, "and you can't even do that right. You never saw Buck Shelford cry, did you? Now there was a sportsman."

"Buck Shelford got his scrotum ripped open on the field in 1986," Cara pointed out, her voice rising. "The year prior, it was a crime to be gay, but not to sexually assault your spouse. As a lawyer, your hankering for the good old days leaves something to be desired."

"That's not the point," Edward roared, spittle forming at the corners of his mouth, all decorum gone.

"It's exactly the point," she yelled back. Jesus, she was behaving like a toddler, but the *fire* in her veins as this toxic excuse for a man tried to pile all of his horseshit onto Finn, to shame his own son for showing his emotions, burned her alive from the inside. "You think we got the highest male youth suicide rate in the Western world by telling men to muscle up and bottle their emotions in?" She shook her head, a bitter laugh slipping out. "Your son is incredible. He's smart and caring and generous. Plus, he's *fucking good at his job*. And all of that is a testament to his strength of character, because he sure as shit didn't get any of it from you." She shoved her chair back with a scrape. "Come on, Finn. We're leaving."

Her best friend stood and took the hand she stretched out towards him.

"You can call tomorrow to apologise to him," Cara told Edward. With her other hand, she reached out and snagged the open champagne bottle from the ice bucket. "We're taking this."

She strode out, the slap of her sandals a rapid percussion on the polished floorboards, Finn's softer tread echoing hers on the off beat as she led him through the halls and out the wide front door to the driveway. They got into the Beemer without saying a word and Finn pulled out onto the leafy street, eyes straight ahead.

Cara clutched the cool neck of the champagne bottle a little tighter as he navigated through one of Auckland's upper-class suburbs, Finn's silence hanging like the sword of Damocles over her head. She didn't regret putting Edward in his place, but she hoped she hadn't upset Finn any further. Her fists clenched every time she thought about his father's words, about Edward's eyes flat with toxicity as he sat smugly on his high and mighty throne of white colonial patriarchy.

"Are you angry with me?" Her voice sounded very small in the silence.

Beside her, Finn grunted and flicked on his indicator, turning into a quiet side street. "You didn't need to do that."

Cara's stomach lurched. "I know. But I couldn't let-"

"You didn't need to do that," he interrupted, pulling the car to a stop in a small, deserted park reserve area. *Is he going to leave me here?* "But I'm glad you did."

"Oh." Cara breathed a sigh of relief.

"You're impulsive and fierce and you speak before you think when you're angry," he continued, and her stomach sank. "Now," Finn said, cutting the engine and fixing her with that fathomless ocean blue stare, "get over here and sit on my cock so I can show you how much I appreciate that about you."

CARA LOOKED at him like he was crazy. Maybe he was. Maybe the emotion roaring through his veins was madness. It felt like love, but the two had been confused in the past by men much more intelligent than him. All he knew was that he'd never felt so grateful to another person in his adult life. Grateful for opportunities, of course, but not for a single individual. But then, nobody had ever defended him so passionately before - not him as a person. And to do so to his parents, in their home? The home that was a spectre shadowing every move he'd made since the age of eleven? She was incredible.

"Don't make me ask again, Cara. Get over here."

She flicked a nervous gaze out the window.

"They're tinted," he reminded her, reading the wariness in her face. "I'd never do anything to put you at risk, honey. I only want to make you feel good. Come here and let me do that."

"Is this because I yelled at your dad?" She sounded curious, as though she still expected him to scold her, but she was moving, sliding her underwear down her legs, and it was all he could do not to explode in his pants. *Speaking of...*

"It's because you're a goddess," Finn told her, sliding his seat back and unbuttoning his shorts. "You drive me out of my mind. It doesn't matter if you're shouting at my parents or crying at movies or playing godawful music in my kitchen. I can't get enough of you."

She snorted lightly as she clambered over the centre console. "A goddess indeed."

"You are." He reached out and clasped her hips, helping

her to settle on his lap. "This isn't going to be graceful," he warned her as his aching cock pulsed against her warm flesh. "It's gonna be messy and fast and real. Because that's us, honey. Real." Finn crushed his lips against hers, sweeping inside and groaning as she tangled her tongue with his.

"Yeah?" Cara breathed when she pulled back, her eyes like molten chocolate as she reached between them and grasped his stiff flesh.

"Yeah," he gasped, pressing his forehead to hers. "Put me in, Cara. I'm dying for you."

She sank down onto him, warm heat searing his cock. *Mine.*

"Tell me something else that's real," she whispered against his lips, and he chuckled wryly. She wanted an example? He had hundreds.

"The night of your twenty-fifth birthday when the Knights gave us free tickets to the Sydney Smoke exhibition match at Eden Park? You hooked up with one of their players at the aftermatch function." He kissed her again, hard, his lips punishing her for her unknown transgression. "I've bet a hundred bucks against them every time they've played since."

"That's crazy," Cara gasped as he moved his hips, a slow, thorough piston, pressing upwards at the end, holding her hips down on his to take every inch.

"No. What's crazy is that every time they make me money, I donate it to a charity in your name, because you're the reason I'm making it. You and that lucky Aussie prick who got you for one night when I'd spent two years by then praying for you to kiss me in a dark hallway and climb into a taxi with me at the end of the night." He pulsed again, and her head fell back, exposing the creamy column of her throat for his lips.

"Why didn't you say anything?"

"Why didn't you already know?" Finn groaned into her

neck. "Why don't you still? You're the reason for everything I do."

There were no words after that, only sensations. The hot slip and slide of her as she worked him, the wrenching pulls of desire across his lower back that spread down to tug at his balls. The harsh pants that filled the car, along with the scent of raspberries, sweetness and sex mingled in a sharp sweat-edged musk that drove Finn to the edge of insanity as he bucked into the woman of his dreams, claiming her with an almost brutal fervour. Unspoken words danced along the edge of his tongue. *I've been dying to do this since the day I laid eyes on you.*

"Finn," she cried, high and needy, and satisfaction surged through him as her legs started to shake around his hips. Then she was coming, the hot clench of her pussy working him in long, sultry draws as evidence of her orgasm trickled down the sides of his cock like liquid fire.

"Cara," he bellowed, exploding beneath her and she held his head to her damp chest as he flew through the stars, seeing nothing, feeling everything as he poured himself into her.

"Oh my god," he groaned as the last tremors faded and his skin buzzed with lazy pleasure. "Everyone thinks you're such a nice girl."

Cara laughed, and he fell into the sound, letting it wash over him in a rich wave that warmed his heart and his blood.

They put themselves to rights slowly, cocooned in a slow, post-coital haze that shouldn't have been possible in a vehicle, but it was because it was them. He drove them back into the city and pulled up near a boutique ice-cream parlour that specialised in allergen-free flavours since they'd walked out of his parents before dessert. He got a cup of a strawberry-coconut-lime blend and sat in the passenger seat to eat it, the champagne bottle between his ankles. Cara drove his car home, licking at her chocolate-boysenberry waffle cone, the breeze from the open window ruffling her hair like bronze ribbons across her shoulders. Every mile that passed between them and his parents' house relaxed him further, and he sank into the leather seat and closed his eyes.

"Until I was eight, I had a nanny called Betty," he said finally as they crossed the North Shore bridge, and Cara reached over to turn down the stereo, Brandon Flowers' vocals settling into the background hum of the engine and the wind.

"Was she a good nanny?" Cara asked carefully. He knew she was well aware of the hierarchy and politics of live-in childcare, thanks to her sister Izzy's work as an au pair.

"She was the best." Finn smiled as the memories floated back. "When I was about six, I got obsessed with The Wishing Tree. You know, that Enid Blyton book where the chair had wings on its legs and it flew kids to different magical lands?"

Beside him Cara was already nodding. "God, yes. I loved Enid Blyton. One summer, Izzy and I renamed our dog Timmy and refused to drink anything but ginger beer. We pretended our neighbours were running a smuggling ring and watched them across the paddock with a pair of binoculars for a fortnight."

"The Famous Five?" Finn asked and grinned when she nodded again. "Who were you?"

Cara snorted. "Anne. I wanted to be George, but Izzy claimed her."

"That makes sense."

"Easy for a Julian to say."

They smirked at each other good-naturedly before he continued. "Betty was kind of like that. One day I came home from school and she'd taped red wings to the bottom of one of the dining room chairs. I sat in it and she picked the whole thing up and whizzed me all over the property. She'd hidden little treasures everywhere - a troll doll in the pool house and a matchbox car in the gardens, and she had stories made up for every location. We ended up in my bedroom and she'd made a fort out of bedsheets and pillows and we curled up there and read a collection of short stories about our adventures from the day, like a bunch of Finn and the Wishing Chair shorts with pictures she'd drawn. It must have taken a couple of weeks to set the whole thing up."

"She sounds amazing."

"She was." He smiled. "Pretty much every good memory from my childhood has Betty in it somewhere. On my birthday she used to let me choose what kind of cake I wanted, and then we'd make and decorate it together. Mum and Dad always ordered me a fancy looking one from a bakery for my birthday party, but the cakes I made with Betty were what we ate on my actual birthdays."

"Why didn't she stay until you went to boarding school?"

Finn's heart twisted in his chest, the familiar pull of guilt and sadness that came whenever he thought about Betty, about how much she'd meant to him. He stabbed his spoon into the melting lump of his ice cream.

"I was behind with my maths homework, a couple of weeks worth. It was my own fault. I was lost with the material, so I lied and said I didn't have any. I was still doing homework for my other subjects, so it wasn't too obvious. Anyway, my teacher called my parents. They went apeshit. They sat Betty and I down after dinner and had a go at her, saying she wasn't doing her job right, that I was going to be held back and it was all her fault. All bullshit of course, but I didn't know that then. I said it wasn't her fault, but they weren't listening."

"They fired her because you were behind in maths?" Cara's outrage was clear.

"Nope." Finn shook his head. "They fired her because I said I loved her. I got so angry with the way they blamed her, I stood up and yelled back at them. I said that Betty was my favourite person in the whole world and I loved her and they couldn't talk to her like that." He paused, the memory pressing heavily on him, leaking a cold worm of guilt and anger into the warm car. "They sent me to bed and I never saw her again. The next day Vera was there and she stayed until I went to boarding school." *Until the incident.* "She was nice enough, but she never played with me. She made sure I did my homework, cooked dinner for me and read me one story a night. Non-fiction, usually." She'd given him that at least, a curiosity about the real world, its people and places.

"Oh, Finn," Cara breathed. "Did you ever look for Betty?"

He nodded, his throat tight. "Yeah. But that's about the extent of what I know about her. Her first name and the fact that she nannied for a few years in her early twenties. Not a lot to go on. Eight-year-olds don't think much about how to track people down on the Internet." He paused. "Well, I didn't, at least." *Not then.* "I still think about her, though. Especially when I'm at the house." He shook his head, frustrated. "I think about how that was the first time I stood up to my parents, and lost someone I loved. That's been the pattern. Everything and everybody I love, they find a way to taint it."

A warm hand landed on his thigh and squeezed. "For what it's worth," Cara said, her voice firm. "I think she loved you too. And I think she'd be really proud of the man you are today."

"You do?"

"Of course. And I hope you're proud of yourself. You, Finn Chalmers, are incredible."

Back at home, Cara made good on her promise and they

watched *1917*, curtains pulled against the bright sunshine, the two of them and Ted enveloped in their own world.

"I needed this," he murmured as the credits rolled, brushing her hair back to press a kiss against her forehead.

"You needed to tell your parents to fuck off?" Cara yawned, snuggling deeper into his arms. "I agree."

A smile tugged at Finn's lips. "Smart arse," he whispered fondly. "I needed you. I needed us, the way we are now. I feel like I've been floating until this point, but you anchor me."

"I drag you down?" Cara asked, but he felt her smile against his chest.

"You keep me steady," he countered. "You always have. But now? Being with you is like discovering how to breathe again."

Other words, little ones, powerful ones, danced on the tip of his tongue, but she'd stilled in his arms, her spine a steel rod that he softened gently, stroke by stroke. He held them back, settling instead on the truth.

"You're my best friend."

Cara's shoulders lowered, and she exhaled, her breath brushing across the fabric of his shirt in a loose gust.

"You're my best friend, too." She whispered the words against the thick cotton weave covering his chest and he felt them land one by one on his heart, settling there. An unbreakable bond. An unspoken promise. This was the core of them. Finn knew it like he knew the texture of the ball in his hand, the smell of liniment, the sight of the sun rising over the estuary from his porch. If they were never more than this, it would be enough. He could live without being Cara Holt's lover. He could never live without being her friend. If he was ever forced to choose between the two, he'd take Sundays snuggled on the couch watching movies over warming her bed any day of the week. But selfishly, he hoped he never had to choose. Instead, he hoped they could stay suspended in time at this blissful intersection of friends and lovers long enough that her doubts and fears would dissipate. Dandelion seeds tossed and scattered in the wind by the depth of his love.

This was enough. But that? That, Finn decided, as Cara's breath evened into a sleep-steady rhythm, would be everything to him.

CHAPTER 10

"*Y*ou're a poopyheady!"

"No, you're a poopyhead!"

It must be a full moon, Cara thought as she watched Magda hurry over to intervene in the escalating drama over in the reading nook. *These kids are off the wall.*

The last two weeks had flown by in a blur. Finn appeared to have shaken off the nervous emotion of the first preseason game and played a blinder last weekend under the trial captaincy of veteran forward Victor Hewitt. The media had covered the story of his tears at the initial press conference for a couple of days before dropping it to focus on a soccer player caught running a dogfighting ring. He hadn't heard from his parents as far as she knew, but he'd declined an invitation to a charity event his mother was involved in when it arrived. She'd only noticed because she'd spied the invitation on the counter and noted the foundation name. She'd accompanied Finn to their galas in the past and knew it was one Helena expected him to attend. Instead, a hefty signed cheque lay next to it and he'd stopped on their way into town one morning to drop a gilded envelope into a post-box. Since the blow-up at his parents' place, they'd spent their evenings walking Ted along the beach behind Finn's property, joining Manu and Clare at their local pub quiz or going to barre class.

"He's really improving", the instructor had whispered to Cara after their last class, and Cara had chosen not to tell her that Finn claimed the extra focus on flexibility would cement him as 'the greatest lover she had ever known.' That was a direct quote, and damned if the man wasn't doing his best to prove it true. Most nights she came screaming with him inside her, and the nights she didn't they shared bubble baths in his huge slate grey bathroom, watching the sun dip behind the horizon in a slow parade of bronze fire, before snuggling up in bed and talking until they fell asleep. And every night, without fail, Finn held her hand as she drifted off.

He could rest easy. The title of Cara Holt's Greatest Lover was his.

"Cara?" Denise popped her head through the door to the main room. "You have a delivery."

Weird. Though she *had* hit up the latest Scholastic book catalogue for a few items to donate to the children's hospital.

It wasn't books though. It was a stunning floral display in a heavy glass vase, a riot of roses, tulips and snapdragons in pinks and reds, all interspersed with native ferns. It was gorgeous. Elegant, romantic, and lush. The prettiest bouquet she'd ever seen.

"Who's sending you flowers?" Denise leant on her crutches in the office doorway eyeing the delivery appreciatively. Heat crawled up Cara's neck as she searched for a suitable response.

"Uh, I…"

"Finn, huh?" Denise asked, click-clacking her way to her chair and flopping down in it, stowing the crutches under the desk. "'Bout time."

"What? No!" Cara spluttered, giving up when she saw the knowing look Denise levelled at her. "How'd you guess?"

"No need to guess," Denise replied. "Everything about the man screams good sex. If I had even a passing interest in dick, I'd climb him like a tree."

"Nice," Cara drawled and Denise shrugged.

"Can't blame a lesbian for looking. The fact it took you this long to jump on board Finn's welcome wagon is on you. You must have had those best friend blinders on."

"They were working just fine," Cara grumbled, plucking the card out of the teeming mass of blooms.

"And now he's working you over just fine?"

"Stop it," Cara laughed. "Does Jodie know you have a non-sexual crush on my best friend?"

"Jodie agrees with me. She wants to ask him to be a topless waiter at her hen's do. Said it would look like a classical painting was pouring body shots onto her."

"I can't believe you found someone even weirder than yourself to marry," Cara muttered as she unfolded the plain card.

You look very pretty today.

She did not, actually, look very pretty today. She rarely did by half past two in the afternoon. There was green paint smeared across the front of her navy tee - she'd long since given up wearing pastels to work - and strands of ginger hair were sticking to the back of her neck where they'd come loose from her braid. She had specks of glitter meandering up one arm and Play-Doh caked under her chipped nails.

Smiling at the sweetness of the gesture, she snapped a quick picture of the bouquet and sent it to Finn with a smiley face.

"I don't know though," she sighed, slipping into the other office chair. Magda and the student teacher would be okay for a few minutes. "I don't know where this is going."

Beside her, Denise started humming The Wedding March, and Cara rolled her eyes.

"It's definitely not going there. I love Finn, and I love you and Jodie, and my sister, but romantic love isn't for me. What happens when I move back to my flat? Do we go back to being just friends? Friends with benefits? And what happens when he finds someone he has actual feelings for?"

"Romantic love isn't for you? Why are you my bridesmaid then?" Denise popped open the jar of protein balls and fished one out.

"That's different. I'm for it for other people, but I don't want to be *in love*. I don't want my happiness dependent on somebody else, on their moods and behaviour. I definitely wouldn't be happy in a relationship with someone who has as much money as Finn does." Cara lifted a hand to her chest, anxiety pulling tight across her breastbone at the idea of it. "We're from different worlds. He's practically made of cash and I flat with three other girls in a place with bugger all insulation and black mould growing in the bathroom. It's fine because we're friends and I always pay my own way, but that level of disparity in a relationship?" She shuddered. "Can you imagine?"

"Can I imagine moving out of a shitbox flat that's destroying my health to move in with a hot pro athlete who'll give me countless orgasms and treat me like a queen?" Denise queried. "Yeah. I can. Sounds good, actually."

"Sounds horrific," Cara countered firmly. "Inequality like that is always going to breed discontent, a layer of reliance or expectation that leads to resentment."

"Babe." Denise shook her head. "You know, I think you're great, but you sound unhinged right now."

Cara opened her mouth to protest, but her phone beeped. She picked it up and swiped to open Finn's message.

Nice flowers. Where did they come from?

Cara's stomach churned as she hit the call button.

"Hello?"

"You didn't send the flowers?"

"No." She could hear the frown in his voice through the phone. "When did they arrive?"

"A few minutes ago."

"And they're addressed to you?"

"Yes. There was a card."

"What does it say?" His words were tight, and in the background Cara could hear the thud and crash of weights hitting the floor.

"It says I look pretty today," she said, her voice small. She'd been so sure the flowers had been from Finn, but there hadn't been any reason to think so. He'd never sent her flowers before.

How could I be so stupid? The entire reason she was staying with Finn, the entire reason they were navigating the slippery gauntlet from best friends to whatever-this-was, was because there was somebody watching her.

Over the phone, a door slammed and the background noise disappeared.

"I'm coming to get you," Finn said, his voice firm.

"I'm still working," she protested.

"No, she's not," Denise called towards the phone. "She's not leaving the office until you get here."

"Thank you, Denise," Finn replied. Then - "*Shit!*"

"What? Finn? Are you okay?" Her heart beat a rapid staccato in her chest.

"I'm fine," his voice said grimly in her ear. "But somebody's chucked a brick through my windshield."

～

THE FLUORESCENT BULB FLICKERED, casting a twitchy shadow across the cold linoleum of the police station waiting room. Finn jiggled his knee, tense and frustrated as he shifted on the unforgiving bench awaiting Detective Pring. Beside him, Cara was as quiet and withdrawn as she'd been since he pulled up to her workplace in a taxi and she'd slid the offensive bouquet across the backseat to him before buckling in for their ride to Auckland's central police station. He'd busied himself on the ride, making calls; to request his car be towed and repaired, to the Knights management to report the security breach. His own evidence lay at his feet now, a brick he'd wrangled from the front seat of the Beemer with a note wrapped around it that read *I know your secrets.*

What secrets? The time he'd got pissed on a rugby trip in the under 19's and woken up naked in bed with two of his teammates in the same condition? The abortion he'd driven his cousin to when she'd called him at sixteen sobbing over a positive test and a shitty boyfriend? None of those were illegal, nor was he ashamed of them. Until this month, his biggest secret had been his unrequited love for Cara, and he wasn't doing a great job of concealing that.

"Miss Holt?"

Finn's head jolted up at the voice, as did Cara's next to him. Detective Pring stood in the doorway leading to the rest of the station, his mouth a solemn line. "Please follow me. You too, Mr Chalmers."

They trailed behind him down a long corridor, Cara with her flowers and him with his brick, both wearing thin latex gloves she'd filched from preschool. Detective Pring led them to a small but tidy office, almost sterile save for the single hand drawn picture of three people standing under a giant sun carefully pinned to a bulletin board next to lists of procedures and posters about the importance of restorative justice.

Cara noticed it immediately. "You have kids?"

The detective glanced at the picture. "One. I used to have a photo of her in here, but a gang member threatened to murder her so I took it down."

Cara blinked. "Fair enough," she murmured faintly.

"Now," Pring said, turning back towards them. "I'll need to take your statements regarding today's incidents."

The statements took forever, both of them combing through the minute details of their day, from their joint drive into the city from the North Shore that morning to their shared taxi ride to the station. Detective Pring interrupted often, fact checking or asking for further detail as he typed, and Finn was exhausted by the time the clock hit six and they wrapped up.

"Obviously," the detective said, placing the printed statements in front of them to sign, "the stalker's behaviour has escalated, and they've also become aware of your relationship with each other. You're being careful with security at the house?" He directed the question to Finn, who nodded, even as he ran through in his mind additional measures he might take.

"Good," the detective said. "I have to be honest, Miss Holt, it seems you're most accessible at work. Is there any way you might stay home for a few days?"

Cara was already shaking her head. "I can't."

"You can," Finn argued, his blood heating at the idea she would head straight back into an unsafe environment.

"I can't," Cara repeated through gritted teeth. "I don't have enough leave."

"Who cares about your leave? Just take time off."

"I can't afford to," she ground out. "I'm still paying rent at the flat, even though I'm not there right now. I have bills to pay. I can't take unpaid time off. I used up the last of my sick days with the migraine and my new allocation doesn't kick in until Easter."

"Fuck the allocation," Finn barked. "I'll pay your rent. Tell me how much you need."

A pink flush climbed Cara's neck. "You will not."

"Cara," Finn replied. "Come on. I have the money."

"I'm not taking your money, Finnegan," she snapped, cheeks flaming red now. "Suggest it again, and I'll move right back into my flat."

"I only want to help," he protested, frustration sharpening his words.

"You *are* helping," she argued. "You're letting me stay with you. That's generous enough, especially considering you've now put yourself in the firing line." She gestured at the brick on the desk in front of them.

Detective Pring cleared his throat, drawing their attention.

"I'm sorry, Miss Holt," he said. "But Mr Chalmers is right. Going back to work now would be foolish. To be honest, I'd recommend leaving town entirely for a few days now that your stalker is aware of your relationship. And you, Mr Chalmers, would probably be wise to leave your home for a few days as well. Now we have the flowers to go on, we'll likely wrap this case up quickly. In the meantime, we can commit some extra constables to patrolling the area around your house to ensure all your safety measures are effective and to deter anyone who isn't supposed to be there."

Finn was already nodding. "That's fine. We can move out. Maybe a hotel-"

"No," Cara interrupted. "No, I can leave town for a few days." She bit her lip, clearly doing calculations in her head. "I can go to Taranaki, stay with my parents for a day or two."

"How will you get there?" Finn asked.

"I can drive."

"The fuck you can," he snorted. "Not in that death-trap on wheels you call a car."

"Leave my car alone."

"I wish *you'd* leave it alone. On the side of the road somewhere."

"Well, what do you suggest?" She was clearly fed up with him.

"Look," he reached out and took her hand, trying very hard to ignore Detective Pring, who faked extreme interest in the ceiling fan. Finn rubbed his thumb over the tender inside of Cara's wrist, back and forth, a slow slide over her pulse point. "I know you're not happy about this, but it's the best solution. Let me pay your rent, just for the next month," he hastened to add when she opened her mouth to argue. "Use your money to fly south and give the detectives a chance to find this person. You can think of it as a loan if you like."

Cara narrowed her eyes at him. "I'll pay you back."

"If that's what you want," he assured her smoothly. "But please don't let your pride get in the way of your safety. You know your car isn't reliable for a ten hour round trip. It might make it, but it might not either. And then you're stranded somewhere on State Highway Three with no phone service and a car needing expensive repairs."

She pursed her lips. "I'm not happy about this," she warned.

"I know, but you can be unhappy and still know it's the right thing to do."

He held his breath as he waited for her response, exhaling gustily when she nodded.

"Okay. Thank you, I guess."

"Thank *you*." He gripped her hand tighter.

They farewelled Detective Pring and headed back to the waiting room, where Finn called a taxi. Cara booked her flight to Taranaki on the drive back across the Harbour Bridge, the evening sun picking up glints of copper in her hair as she typed and he watched her from the corner of his eye, relaxing into the knowledge that she might be leaving him for a few days, but she'd be safe.

"When should I book my return flight for?" she inquired, facing him, and he took the opportunity to brush a strand of hair behind her ear.

"Friday afternoon? That's three nights if you're leaving tomorrow. Hopefully everything will be sorted by the time you get back. The cops have more evidence now, and they'll pull everything from the security footage at Knights' Stadium. You should be okay by then." And maybe, selfishly, he wanted her back by then too. Back in his arms. Back in the family box for the game on Saturday.

"Okay," she murmured, tapping away at her phone. "Would you be able to pick me up from the airport? I can get an Uber there in the morning."

"Sounds good."

"What about you?" she asked as her phone pinged with her flight confirmation email. "Are you going to stay at the house?"

"Nah. I'll ask Manu and Clare if I can hole up in their spare room for a couple of nights." He wasn't worried about security at his place, but he didn't need to tempt some arsehole into trying anything funny, either. Plus, without Cara there, his house wouldn't feel like home. Now that she'd been there for more than a couple of nights, she'd stamped her presence on his residence like she'd stamped herself on his soul. Her sneakers sat by the front door, her book on a side table, her raspberry scent haunting the hallways of his home. Her dog curled on his couch.

"I'll take Ted with me," he said. "He can be a city dog for a couple of days. I'll take him to cafes and order him wanky puppuccinos."

Her eyes crinkled at the corners as she smiled at the thought. "He'll love it."

"He'll miss you," Finn said. "I will too."

"I'll miss you too." Her voice was so soft he barely heard it, but her words settled around him, sweet and reassuring, and threads of hope wound their way into his heart, wrapping tight at the possibility that once all of this was over, they could move forward. Together.

He just had to survive the next three days without her.

CHAPTER 11

Taranaki was a bad idea. Cara knew it as soon as she'd pulled her rental car to a stop on the gravel driveway in front of the main house. God knows why she'd thought coming back to her parents' house right when she was entangled with her own wealthy love interest had been a decent idea, but it had taken approximately two point eight seconds before she'd realised she was wrong.

That's how long it had taken for her father to wander out of the garage, eye her up as she exited the vehicle and grunt, "What are you doing here then?"

"I'm here to see Mum," she replied, not bothering to soften the truth. She and her father hadn't had one-on-one time since the painful and awkward threats he'd implied after she discovered him naked from the waist down humping Mrs Bridgeman in the barn.

"She's inside," Steve Holt replied, and turned back towards the open garage doors.

"She usually is," Cara muttered under her breath. It took a lot to keep a farm running, and a disproportionate amount of that work happened behind the scenes, in the kitchen and the office. Both her mother's domain, however much her father might like to claim the business side of things for himself.

Cara let herself in without knocking. Her childhood home was the same as ever. A single-storey villa that had sat on the land since her great-great-grandfather had first built it at the beginning of the last century. Four bedrooms, two bathrooms, two living rooms and a mudroom, all in keeping with the historical aesthetic of the home, and then the kitchen. Gleaming countertops, sleek appliances and cheery yellow walls that complemented the cornflower blue curtains hanging at the above-sink window that looked out on a rambling English cottage-style garden. Her mother was at the counter, dressing a lamb leg for roasting.

"Hey, Mum," Cara said softly, leaning in the doorway.

Linda Holt turned with a gasp.

"Cara!" Her mother hustled across for a hug, trusty apron in place over a chambray shirt and jeans, silver hair cut short, oily hands held aloft. Cara wrapped her arms around her mother and breathed in the familiar scent of Pears soap and roses.

"What are you doing here?" Linda asked, moving towards the sink and rinsing her hands under a stream of water.

"I have a few days off and I thought I'd pop down and visit. Is it okay if I stay for a couple of nights?" Cara let her eyes drift around the light-filled room. There was a new picture of Izzy on the refrigerator - in Croatia maybe? Sunlight bounced off her sister's blonde hair as she stood with her back to a cerulean sea, wearing a long black tank dress, flip flops and a smile.

"Of course it is," Linda assured her. "Flick the kettle on and we can have a nice cup of tea and a chin wag. You can tell me all about what you've been up to since Christmas."

"Christmas was only six weeks ago, Mum," Cara grinned.

She might dislike coming home, but she loved her mother like crazy. It was the only explanation for why she'd kept her father's dirty secret for so long.

"Six weeks is plenty of time to get into mischief." Linda rummaged in the pantry and pulled out a container of dark brown biscuits. She grabbed a handful and slapped them on a plate. Cara noted the white nubs of small nuts baked into the top of them.

Peanut brownies, yum.

"How's work then, if you've not got any scandalous titbits for me?" Linda asked, and Cara gave her a rundown of the preschool's activities - the new initiatives the sector was being told to adopt without time or resources to do so, Denise's sprained ankle, Magda's weird new habit of eating sardines on toast at their morning meetings. She deliberately left out any mention of the anonymous deliveries and the fact that she'd been living with Finn. Her mum was a world class worrier - even now when Cara or Izzy took an international flight they needed to message her once they landed to assure her they'd not been killed in a fiery crash en route to their final destination.

After she'd thoroughly bored her mother with a rant against the Ministry of Education officials who'd never set foot in a teaching space, she unloaded her small suitcase into her old bedroom. The walls were sadly bereft of the fairy lights and artistically arranged Polaroids of her high school friends and instead painted a calming eggshell, more in keeping with its new life as a guest room. Out of curiosity, Cara poked her head into Izzy's room next door. Stacks of unpacked boxes towered like giant Jenga pieces. On the bed lay an unstructured collage of postcards from around the world, a crime novel perched on the bedside table, and by the full-length mirror a pair of sneakers lay in the corner. At only twenty-five, almost the same age as Finn, Izzy flitted back into New Zealand when it suited her, staying at their parents until another overseas job came up or she'd saved enough to set off on some intrepid hike to Machu Picchu or across Portugal. She'd left town the moment she finished high school, never looking back and although Cara was thrilled for her sister that she'd been spared the responsibility that came with running herself ragged trying to make sure everyone else was taken care of, a small part of her selfishly wished she could have the luxury of only chasing her own dreams too.

Isn't that what you're doing now? A voice whispered in her head as she left the house and went to the stables. *Isn't this thing with Finn just for you? A chance for you to put your own wants first and worry about the consequences later? You know it can't last, but you want what you can get while the going is good.*

Frowning, she shook her head, trying to shake the intrusive thought away, but it stayed with her, a nagging sense of disquiet in the back of her mind as she tacked up her favourite mare and set out at an easy canter along the west boundary line.

So what if I am? she asked herself as she reached the river cutting through the north-west corner of the farm. Sun dappled water danced and burbled its way over rocks, glinting like a sea of diamonds. The river had changed since she was here last, as rivers did; silt and sand and rocks moving with the passing of the seasons and the liquid bounty of the mountains. Each year, an altered terrain emerged and without fail, the river carved its own path through the obstacles to swish and swirl undaunted through the fields and out to the Tasman Sea.

It won't end well, her pessimistic inner voice taunted. *It can't, not with a man like that. With his money? His status? He might be your best friend, but ultimately he'll go back to his casual-*

dating roster of models and athletes and you'll be at home on your couch, in your sweatpants, covered in chip crumbs.

As if hearing her thoughts, her steed, Pepper, snorted and shifted under her.

"What do you reckon, Peps?" Cara leaned forward and stroked her hand down the warm silk of the horse's neck. "You reckon he means all the lovely things he says to me? Or is this par for the course? Am I stupid to let him charm me?"

Pepper pawed at the ground.

"Yeah, fair point," Cara conceded. "I'm pretty sure your boyfriend bangs about thirty other mares a year too. Men, aye? Can't trust them." Clicking her tongue, she manoeuvred them left to follow the riverside trail upstream. It would take her about forty minutes to circumnavigate the farm boundary. She'd be back in time to help her mum get the rest of dinner ready.

She felt better after her ride, the sweet scent of hay filling her nostrils as she untacked Pepper and groomed her quickly before popping the horse back in her stall and rewarding her with a carrot from the small tack room fridge. It had taken six months before she'd been able to set foot in the stables after discovering her father's affair - every time she'd tried, the familiar sights and sounds brought memories of that awful day rushing back to her and she'd hurry nauseous from the threshold. She'd been so angry with her father - was still so angry with him, high and mighty on his throne of deceit, acting every bit the hardworking husband and loyal companion to her mother when Cara knew the truth - his fidelity was an illusion and so were his morals. Threatening to take part of her mother's farm if they divorced? To carve up the estate her ancestors had purchased from the local iwi in the years following the signing of the Treaty of Waitangi and portion himself out a slice he'd had no hand in building? The *nerve* of the man.

Entwined with her anger towards her father was the guilt, always, always the guilt. It didn't matter that she'd worked herself ragged trying to compensate for her own omission of truth. It didn't matter that she'd given up hockey, spent her evenings cleaning and cooking to relieve her mother's burden, that she'd let her friendships slip by the wayside by the end of school so that she wouldn't be tempted to spend her afternoons and weekends elsewhere and give her father further opportunities to betray her mother's trust. None of it helped to ease the gnawing feeling in her gut that she needed to tell Linda. But every time she opened her mouth she remembered her father's words - the picture he'd painted for her of a dingy flat in town, her mother working odd jobs to make ends meet, the farm - both Linda's heritage and security in one - held ransom by Steve if she left him. And so she'd kept her father's secret for almost half her life. Yet as she glimpsed the foaling stall door, her stomach roiled again.

Dinner was a quiet affair. The lamb, studded with garlic and rosemary, melted in her mouth, but she was withdrawn, claiming exhaustion from a busy start of the school year when her mother questioned her. The second day was much of the same - she and Linda went for a long walk in the morning, then baked banana bread for morning tea. Pepper was getting some serious exercise and Cara had braved the fort of boxes in Izzy's room to grab the crime novel from next to the bed, only to set it aside two chapters in when she realised it contained a stalking plot.

Not exactly helpful for taking my mind off things.

Cara and her father skirted each other, both dancing in and out of the kitchen when the other was absent to talk to Linda, who watched them both carefully but said nothing as Cara helped her prepare fresh tuna steaks for dinner.

She was curled up with her replacement read, Anne of

Green Gables, on a couch in the formal living room that caught the mid-morning sun when her mother entered the next day.

"You okay, love?" Linda asked.

"Of course," Cara replied, not trusting herself to look up from her book.

"Mmm." Linda sounded dubious as she moved around the room, running a dust cloth over the piano.

"Do you remember this?" She asked the question suddenly, and Cara lifted her head. Linda was looking at the collection of framed photographs clustered on top of the piano.

"Winning the blue ribbon at Pet Day with Barbeque the lamb?"

"Not that," her mother answered, a smile in her voice. "This one." She plucked up a frame and came to sit beside Cara on the low green leather Chesterfield.

"The first time your dad took you out fishing on your Uncle Bill's boat." She passed the picture to Cara, who looked down at the image of her younger self, maybe seven or eight. She was wearing navy leggings and a purple windbreaker, her hair a tangled mess around her head. In her hand was a piece of fishing line, a lone spotty attached to it, so named for the large dark spot on the female fish's side. If she looked closely, she could see it in the picture still, just above the yellow fin. Beside her stood Steve, clad in a singlet and ridiculously short shorts, both of them beaming with pride at her first catch.

"Yeah," Cara said, her chest tightening. "It was a good day."

Beside her, Linda let out a deep breath. "You know you haven't been home by yourself in a decade? Izzy's always been here when you've visited, or Finn has come with you.

At Christmas the house is full of your cousins. It's been a long time since it was just the three of us here."

"Poor timing, I suppose." Cara forced lightness into her voice.

Linda shook her head slowly. "I don't think that's the case. I think the timing has been extremely deliberate." She paused, and Cara's heart thudded in her ears, instinct warning her to remove herself from the situation. Before she could move though, Linda spoke again.

"What happened between you and your father?"

Oh, Jesus, not now. Not ever, preferably, but especially not now. She should have stayed in Auckland and hoped her stalker dropped off chocolates next. *Anything but this.*

"Nothing," Cara said, and her mother fixed her with a look.

"It's not nothing. Whatever it is, it's kept you from home for the best part of your adult life. You're less than an hour's flight away and we see you maybe twice a year. That's your choice, and I respect it. I'm not asking you to change if that's what makes you feel comfortable, but I am asking you to tell me why."

The roiling sensation in Cara's stomach was back, but this time a metallic tang coated her tongue as well, as though even her mouth was rebelling against letting the truth roll out.

"Mum—"

"The truth, Cara."

Gripping the silver frame until her knuckles whitened, Cara squeezed her eyes shut. There was no way she was going to look at her mother while she shattered her world.

"I caught Dad cheating on you." The six words she had been aching to spill for thirteen years croaked out, as though she'd pulled them from the depths of her consciousness, forcing them into the light against her will. Ugly, painful words, words she should have said earlier, or never have had to say at all, sour in her mouth, passing bitter truth through the air to infect her mother's belief about her marriage.

"Ah," Linda said. "When you were how old?"

"Fourteen."

"Fourteen?" Linda's voice was grim and Cara winced, her eyes still closed. She could hear her mother suck in a deep lungful of air before she spoke again.

"I'm sorry you had to see that. Have you kept it a secret all this time?"

Cara nodded, finally opening her eyes to look at her mother. Linda was staring across the room, jaw tight. "I told Finn a few weeks ago," she admitted. "We were having an argument about paying for things, and I just…I just told him how much it means to me to be financially independent. To support myself so I don't ever end up in a relationship where money is a deciding factor in whether I should stay or go."

Her mother barked out a hollow laugh. "You think money decides that for me?"

"I think," Cara replied carefully, "that money is power. And people who have more than others don't always do the right thing. When I confronted Dad, he told me as much. He told me that if I told you about the affair and you left him, that he'd take the farm. Most of it, anyway. And that you and Izzy and I would be destitute."

"He said that?" Linda's pale brows were near her hairline.

"Yeah. That's why I never let you help me buy a car or pay for uni. I don't want him to have any power over me."

"Since you were fourteen," her mother marvelled, shaking her head. "You poor thing."

"Me?" Cara gave a hollow laugh. "What about you? Who knows if he's still doing it?"

Linda smiled tightly, her gaze still on the ivory flocked wallpaper on the far side of the room. "Oh, he is."

Cara's blood ran cold. "What do you mean?"

Her mother looked at her finally, her brow furrowed over the same brown eyes both of her daughters had inherited.

"I know about his affairs, Cara," she said gently. "I've always known."

Time stood still. A heavy weight thudded in Cara's core and bloomed outward, tightening across her chest. She rubbed a fist against her breastbone, trying to ease the hollow ache.

"What?" she croaked.

Linda nodded, her mouth a grim line.

"But…how?" Cara's voice trembled.

"Your father is many things," Linda said. "But discreet is not one of them."

Her breath caught in her chest, wrenching the tension there tighter, and she fought to inhale past the obstruction.

All these years. All these years and she knew all along.

Her mother was peering at her now. "Cara?" Linda reached for her hand, but Cara jerked away, the open book falling from her grasp to tumble to the floor.

"How could you?" she whispered. "How could you stay with him?"

"I love him," Linda replied simply, and it was the worst sentence Cara could have imagined. Maybe if there had been another reason, some deeper play, she could see why Linda might have stayed in a marriage mired in disrespect and deceit, but *love*? Fickle, flighty love? That flickering emotion that could be doused as easily as candle flame, leaving its victims weak and alone in the dark?

It had done the same to her, her love for her mother leaving her powerless and palsied, stuck in a never-ending cycle of guilt, regret and shame. Only to discover she'd wasted half her life trying to protect someone who never needed it. That she'd given up her own passions in honour of someone else, only to have it thrown back in her face now.

A strangled laugh worked its way out of her. Love. That wily bitch. Well, she wasn't going to suffer under its fantastical illusion ever again.

She stood, scooping up the book and returning it to the ornately carved shelf she'd pulled it from before heading for the door.

"Cara? Are you alright?"

She paused in the doorway at her mother's uncertain tone.

"No. I'm not. I'm leaving."

Linda's mouth dropped open. "Cara, you don't have to—"

"I do. I am. I can't stay here. This house is full of secrets and lies. I don't want any part of it."

"Cara, I swear I never knew he'd asked you to keep it a secret. I'm so angry—"

"What are you going to do? Leave him?" Cara shook her head, too full of rage to regret the sarcastic slant of her words. "You don't get it. It was one thing when I knew how Dad disrespected you, but to realise you knew the whole time…" She met her mother's dark eyes. "I can't stay when I don't respect either of you."

She turned and headed to her bedroom. Her suitcase lay partially packed on the bed, ready for her intended departure after lunch. Scooping up her phone and watch from the bedside table, she tossed them in the open case. Her sleepwear followed, and then she was zipping it up, shoving her feet into her low boots and dragging it through the house. She made a quick pitstop in her bathroom for her toiletries, cramming them into her cross-body bag rather than bothering to open her case again, and then she loaded everything into the backseat of her rental car. She slammed the door and slid into the driver's seat, adrenaline tingling in her fingertips as she started the ignition. In her peripheral vision she saw the front door open, heard her mother call out to her, but she didn't respond, didn't look. Throwing the car into gear, she swerved a wide loop in the driveway, gravel crunching under her tyres as she gunned it down the long drive towards the road back to town. She didn't look back once.

~

"TELL ME YOU'RE JOKING." Cara's words were slow and deliberate as she took in the luxury SUV that sat topped with a big red bow in Finn's driveway.

"Your safety isn't a joke to me," he said firmly, and she gave him a look that could quell a bushfire. She'd been quiet on the drive back from the airport, only saying that her trip had been draining and he'd let her sit in peace, knowing how stressful being back at the farm must be for her in the wake of her knowledge about Steve's infidelity.

"My safety-" she enunciated carefully and, he'd known her long enough to know that was her default when she was overcome with rage but fuck it, he wasn't backing down "-is not your concern, and certainly not your responsibility."

Bullshit.

"Bullshit," he said, and her brows flew to her hairline. "You want me to pretend this isn't serious, that some fucking nutbar isn't *actively stalking you,* and you can just carry on carpooling and flitting around at work like you're not in danger? Like your car isn't a goddamn death-trap waiting to happen. Even without the fact that someone could break into it in the time you take to pop into the shop for an ice-cream, it's not safe. It could break down at any time. Your tyres are fucked, and the car's held together with duct tape and prayers. You need to be safe. *I* need you to be safe, and if that means you're pissed off at me for a bit then I can take that. What I cannot take is another day of watching you put yourself at risk just so you can claim that you're independent. Your independence isn't worth shit if you're not safe."

"So this is your solution?" Cara drawled sarcastically, a sour note to her voice he'd never heard before. "You buy my safety? Did you think it would be enough to buy *me*? That I'd be so overwhelmed by your generosity I'd throw myself at you in gratitude?"

It might have crossed my mind. He knew better than to speak the thought aloud.

"I'm not one of your charities." Her voice dripped with scorn. "You can't splash money at my problems and expect a pat on the back and a shiny plaque in your honour."

"That's not what I'm doing."

"That's what you always do! Every time a problem comes up, you paper over it with money and charm. But I'm not a problem to be solved, Finn. I don't want to be saved."

"You're not being reasonable," he replied calmly.

"Fuck reasonable!" she shouted, and he took a step back, surprised by the force of her words. "It's not reasonable for you to try and buy me like some second-rate whore. I will not be indebted to you! Not to anyone!"

"It's a gift," he protested. "You already accepted rent money. What's the big deal about this?"

Her brown eyes narrowed dangerously. "That's what you think? Now you've hooked me into some kind of debt with you, you can just keep adding to it? Keep me linked to you forever?"

"Is that so bad?" Frustration simmered in his blood. "For us to be linked?"

"With *money*?" Her scorn was palpable. "Absolutely."

"Why can't you just let me provide you with something you need, no strings attached?"

"So it doesn't have GPS? There's no way for you to know where I am when I'm in this car?"

He stuttered. "Well, of course it has GPS."

"Is it in my name?"

"I needed it in mine for the insurance. I can put it in yours if it's important to you."

"No strings attached, huh?" Cara's laugh bordered on hysterical. "This thing is fucking macrame tying me to you."

"What's wrong with that?" He was shouting too. "What's wrong with being connected to me?"

"I'm not some girl who needs you to look after her. I can do just fine on my own."

"I don't want you to be on your own! I want you to be with me!"

"Why?" She threw her hands in the air. "Why is this so important to you?"

"Because I love you," he roared, and she stepped back, brown eyes wide. Silence fell between them, heavy in the wake of his shouted confession.

"Of course you do." Her voice was quieter now, edged with hesitancy. "We're friends."

Finn shook his head, chest rising and falling like he'd run a marathon. Perhaps he had - perhaps all of this, the years of friendship, loving Cara but never letting her see, had all been some kind of endurance event. Now it was over, he'd crossed the finish line, the words were out there, big and bold in the air above them and whether he emerged victorious or keeled over from the pain to come, he'd done it. He'd told her. Whatever happened now was up to her.

"I'm in love with you, Cara. You can keep the car or chop it into pieces in front of me. I don't give a shit, but don't you dare try to tell me not to take care of you where I can. You'd be better off telling the sun not to rise. You're not mine, not yet, but I'm yours, and there's nothing I won't do to keep you safe. The only things that matter to me are your health and happiness. So be mad at me. Rail and scream and threaten to walk away if that makes you feel better, but when you're finished, this car will still be here waiting for you and so will I."

She glared at him, strands of ginger hair that had escaped her braid stuck to her flushed neck and chest. He readied himself for her rebuttal, but instead, she let out a roar and stomped into the house.

"That went well," he said to Ted, and followed her inside. He found her in the kitchen, a pan heating on the stove while she dug through the fridge.

"I've prepaid a year's insurance on the car," he offered casually, as she ripped open a brand new package of halloumi with a scowl, tossing the entire slab in the pan. "Also, if you're finished being mad, we could talk about this like adults."

She muttered something under her breath he didn't quite catch as she poked at her mound of cheese with a spatula.

"Sure," he commented agreeably. "Being passive-aggressive is fine, too."

"Watch your snark, Finnegan. I'm feeling pretty aggressive-aggressive," she snapped, spinning to face him and folding her arms across her chest.

"Am I in danger of a spanking?" Finn nodded towards the spatula she still held.

"Don't try to be cute." Cara dropped the utensil next to the stove and massaged her temples. "I'm mad at you."

"Right. Why is that again?"

"You can't just buy me a car. I recognise you mean well," she continued, holding up her hand as he opened his mouth to interject, "but it makes me uncomfortable. Aside from that, there's the fact that I *very clearly* told you weeks ago not to do it. Not only did you buy me an extravagant item, you disrespected a decision I'd already made and communicated to you."

"Look, Cara," Finn tried to gentle his voice. "With all due respect, it was the wrong decision."

"Maybe you think so, but it was mine." She turned back to the stove, scooped up the spatula and flipped the contents of the pan. The scent of fried cheese wafted through the air, and Finn's mouth watered.

"When you do that, take my decisions away from me," Cara continued, "it makes me feel like I don't matter. As if I'm irrelevant, like you're not seeing me."

"Honey." Finn's heart twisted in his chest. "You're all I see."

"Then why don't you listen to me?" Her voice broke on the word listen and he was around the counter in a flash, wrapping her in his arms and pulling her against him, her quiet sobs reverberating through her ribcage into his chest.

He held her quietly and let her frustration and anger work its way out in hot tears that landed on his forearms, trickling across his skin to mark maps of his errors in salty streaks.

"Come on," he whispered when the tears slowed. "Come sit with me." He reached past her to turn off the pan and fetched a plate, knife and fork. Sliding the fried brick of dairy onto the plate and holding it and the cutlery in one hand, he grasped Cara's hand with his other one and led her to the couch.

"Eating on the couch?" The love of his life raised an eyebrow at him as she sank into her usual spot, her red-rimmed eyes doing nothing to diminish her sardonic drawl. "You really must feel sorry for me."

"I'm worried for you," Finn responded honestly, and handed her the plate that almost guaranteed constipation in her future.

Better buy some prunes.

"Cara, you're the most important person in my world." He sat down next to her as she sliced off a chunk with her knife and fork. "Of course I want to protect you. As for disrespecting your decision?" He shook his head. "That was never my intention."

"Intentions don't count," she mumbled around a mouthful of halloumi. "Actions do."

"Yeah," Finn nodded. "I know, but I also know about inaction, about what that can cost." He met her eyes and took a deep breath in.

Here we go.

"When I was eleven, we were the victims of a home invasion. Three men broke into our house looking for valuables. Nice house, good neighbourhood, you know how it is. Mum and Dad should have had better security, but back then they didn't. I was still awake when it happened. It was well past my bedtime, but my parents had hosted a dinner party and they'd allowed me to sit in the kitchen with Serena and eat the same fancy meal as them as long as I stayed out of sight. Dad and one of the other partners at his law firm had decided to carry on and head into town to some whisky bar and Serena had gone home, so it was only Mum and me at home when it happened."

"What?" Cara breathed. "Why have you never told me this before?"

"Because it's the worst memory of my life?" He shook his head ruefully, even as she set aside her plate and scooched towards him, her pale hand coming to rest on his forearm.

Her touch gave him strength, and he took another fortifying breath as the memories surged, battering at the corners of his mind where he was fragile.

"I still don't know how they got in. I never asked and nobody ever offered the information. One second it was me and Mum, and the next they were in front of us. One of them had a knife..." he trailed off, the words sticking in his throat.

"Helena's scar," Cara whispered, and he nodded, shame rolling over him in sticky, suffocating waves, pulling his skin tight.

"I was so scared I threw up. Blueberry cheesecake everywhere, down the front of my pyjamas and on the floor. The one with the knife came towards me and Mum got between us, but she slipped on the mess. I don't know if he meant to hurt her, or me, but she got cut as she fell. There was blood all over her face and the men were shouting, running everywhere, opening drawers and looting through stuff while I called emergency services, who couldn't understand me, I was crying so hard."

Warm arms wrapped around him and he leaned into them. He let her lower him until he was lying in her arms, cushioned by his best friend and his comfortable couch, the memory still sharp but safer now. *He* was safer now.

"The invaders left after a few minutes. They took electronics, art, jewellery. All smallish stuff they could carry. They left us there, covered in vomit and blood. I called Dad and told him what had happened and he got there just after the ambulance and the police. They took Mum away, and Dad..." He shook his head, brushing his temple back and forth against the soft swell of Cara's cheek. "Dad barely spoke to me. He couldn't look at me. He sent me to have a shower and get changed into fresh pyjamas, but I couldn't sleep. I heard Mum come home later in the night and I snuck down. They were in his study and..." His breath hitched. "And I heard him say I should have done more to protect her. That I was supposed to be the man of the house when he wasn't there." A hot tear slipped out and ran across the bridge of his nose as he remembered hearing that, hearing the disgust and derision in his father's voice as he hid in the shadows of the hall, the scent of bleach still burning in the air.

"Oh, honey." Cara's voice was heavy with compassion. She smoothed her hand over his hair in long, slow strokes and his breathing evened out to keep time with the motion. "You poor thing. I'm so sorry that happened to you."

"They sent me to boarding school a month later," he mumbled, lulled into peace by her gentle caress. "He barely spoke to me until then. He's barely spoken to me since, to be honest, except to tell me he expected me to study law and go into the firm with him. Mum tried, but it was so hard to look at her. The stitches were so dark and spiky, they were all I could see when we were together. Then I was gone, and we haven't had to be together much at all since."

"You poor, sweet man," Cara murmured again, that endless perfect stroke continuing. "You are worth so much more than that. I hate that I can't go back and fix it for you, take you out of that horrible environment with the people who failed you, over and over again."

"You're with me now," he said, too blissed out to care that honesty was falling like water from his mouth. "It's all been better since you."

"I wish I'd found you sooner." She pressed a kiss to his brow. "If I could go back in time, I'd come find you. I'd leave home the day I discovered my dad screwing around in the barn. I'd come to the city and track you down. It'd be just the two of us, taking care of each other through those horrible years in the wilderness. I would protect you, and you would protect me. Just us. Always."

"You don't even let me protect you now."

Another kiss.

"I'm not talking about a car, which I'm still not accepting, or your enormous gates and cameras, which suddenly make sense." Her hand left his head and travelled down his chest, leaving a warm tingle in its wake until it came to rest on his heart. "I'm talking about here. I'd protect your heart. It's the most valuable thing you have."

The organ in question clenched. "It's yours," Finn told her hoarsely, his eyes closed, exhaustion seeping through him. As he crept towards slumber, he tried not to be disappointed when she didn't say it back.

CHAPTER 12

"**W**hat the fuck is that?"

Clare Esera grinned up at him. "Isn't it great?"

"No," Finn replied, staring horror-struck at the framed black and white portrait of him wiping tears from his eyes with a dark cotton handkerchief. "It's not great. It is decidedly ungreat."

"Don't be silly," Clare said. "It's one of my favourite shots from the entire wedding."

"Then make it your screensaver. Don't hang it in your living room."

"It's a gallery wall," she proclaimed with exaggerated patience. "Nobody is going to notice you."

The scent of raspberries filled the air. "Are you crying in that photo?" Cara asked.

"For fuck's sake," Finn groaned. "Clare, take it down."

"Not a chance, Charming. It took me almost a month to get the composition right." Manu's wife reached up and patted his cheek. "Besides, it's not like you're the primary focus." She gestured to a much larger picture of herself and

Manu in the centre of the display, the Pacific Ocean stretching out for miles behind them as they stood at the edge of a cliff, gazing into each other's eyes. Their wedding in Avali had been gorgeous and while he wasn't ashamed to admit he'd cried like a baby through their vows, he didn't want photographic evidence of it on their living room wall for everyone they knew to see. Especially now that he needed to be above reproach to get the team to believe in him again, to earn their trust back after the disaster of his trial captaincy. Tonight's game, with Dominic Greer at the helm, resulting in a win, tap-danced across his nerves like a live wire. And now this; this display of his weakness framed for the other players to see as they trickled into Manu and Clare's apartment for post-game pizza and beers only heightened his dread.

"Finny!" Dom threw a meaty arm around him. "Great game tonight."

"You too," he replied, trying not to sound churlish. It was true though. For a big man, Dom's evasive style of offence was impressive, particularly given the fact he was pushing thirty.

"You want a beer?"

"No, thanks." Cara already had one in her hand and he never drank if he was going to be driving her. Not a single sip.

Though a night on the orange juice was its own particular form of torture. He had a front-row seat to the action as his friends got rowdier. Not out of control, never that during the season if they could help it, but the looseness that came with being able to relax and wind down in a safe space after a game of hard-fought victory, knowing there were no cameras around, no fans who would run off to the press with a half-cooked story and a blurry photo. By the time they'd emptied the pizza boxes, the room had a giddy atmosphere to it. A sweet nostalgia he was familiar with, that reminded them they all originally played this game for fun, not for the money or the fame. For good times, with good mates. When someone mentioned Truth or Dare, they met it with a resounding cheer.

Most of the players and their partners formed a circle in the living room, while a few who wisely abstained from the game gathered at the dining table with a pack of cards. He could have joined them, but like a homing beacon he was drawn towards Cara, lowering himself onto the floor beside her. She leaned over and rested her head on his shoulder for a moment, and he closed his eyes to savour the way the silk of her hair felt against his jaw. They weren't quite right yet, not after that debacle with the car and his blurted declaration of love, but he knew her signs. She was reaching out to let him know they'd be okay. Finn's battered heart thudded slow and deep in his chest at the unspoken promise. Loving Cara had always been an exercise in patience - first because she didn't know and now while they navigated the tightrope journey from friends to lovers. Expecting her to be on his level straight away was unreasonable. She needed time to learn this new version of him, to reconcile the easy-going, supportive best friend with the worried boyfriend that rose inside him when she was at risk - a product of his own trauma. And he needed to give her that. Even now, when he could barely draw his eyes from her as she straightened and laughed at something that had been said. He was still staring, still soaking her in, when he heard his name.

"Finn, truth or dare?"

"Truth," he answered automatically. Boarding school had taught him never to choose a dare.

"What did you think the first time you saw Cara?"

"What?" He pulled his eyes away from the delicate arch of her foot, her pale pink toenails. "What was that?"

"What did you think about Cara the first time you saw her?" Clare repeated, quirking a dark brow at him. Meaningfully. *Shit, does she know?*

"The first time I saw Cara?" He was stalling, but goddamn, the memory hit him like a punch to the gut.

"Yeah," Clare grinned at him, slow and wicked. *Yeah, she knows.*

"I thought she, um… looked smart."

He could have heard a pin drop.

"Smart?" Cara asked, her voice low and weird.

"Yeah," he shrugged, looking down at the carpet. "You were wearing glasses and real pants, not sweats, even though it was eight in the morning. You sat close to the front, even though nobody else was there." *You looked like all my fantasies come true. You looked like an angel in your floral blouse with your long ponytail. You smiled at me and it felt like the sun coming out after a rainstorm.* "I thought you looked smart."

"You remember my pants?"

"I remember. I didn't wear sweats again for the rest of the semester because I didn't want you to think I was a loser."

Manu laughed, big and booming, cutting through the heavy silence that had settled over the room. "As if your pants would make a difference." He grinned at Cara. "Your turn, Cara."

He could still feel her gaze on him, searching for something, and he kept his eyes down so she wouldn't see the truth scrawled across his face in blazing neon. *I love you.* Finally, thankfully, he felt her attention move elsewhere.

"Dom," she said, overly bright. "Truth or Dare?"

Finn looked up in time to see the huge lock pin her with his eyes. "Dare."

Cara smirked, and *oh shit*, he knew that look. Trouble was coming. "I dare you to come out dancing with me."

"What the hell, Cara?" Finn exploded, but she was still talking, as if he wasn't even there.

"I've been cooped up, Dom. I need a little fun. You'll come dancing with me, won't you?"

The interim captain's eyes flicked to Finn and a faint smile touched the side of his lips. "Sure, Cara. I'll help you have fun. Lads," he raised his voice and every Knight in the room stopped what they were doing and looked his way. "Cara wants to have fun. We're going out dancing. Get organised. I'll have taxis here in thirty minutes."

Finn made a move for Cara immediately, but was waylaid by Rangi Katu petitioning for his nephew's fundraising efforts and by the time he looked up again, she was gone. He pulled out his phone and sent Rangi a thousand bucks for his nephew's fundraiser - fuck knew what he was going to do with five hundred chocolate bars, probably drop them off at the women's shelter. Cara didn't appear again for another twenty minutes, and when she did, *holy hell*. The breath left his body in an almighty exhalation. He felt like he'd been gut-punched. She'd changed out of her jeans and Knights jersey into a black dress Finn vaguely remembered seeing on Clare once, but Cara had six inches on Clare easily, and a slimmer frame. The t-shirt style dress was loose on her but stopped barely short of indecent on her long legs. Then it was miles of pale skin, acres of it, before heeled black ankle boots that he'd barely noticed her wearing at the stadium, but now couldn't take his eyes off. He wanted those heels digging into his back. Finn's mouth watered even as his brain juddered over the thought of her putting herself in danger.

"I need to talk to you," he gritted out, clasping her elbow and leading her out to the little balcony off Manu and Clare's living room.

"What's up?" She shook the curtain of her hair back and he got a good look at her face. She'd put makeup on too, something that made her brown eyes huge and liquid. She looked like sex and sin and salvation. She looked like *his*, and he'd give anything to keep her safe.

"I don't want you to do this." Finn's voice was hoarse.

"Why? It's not *smart*?" There was a bite to her tone, and he silently cursed himself.

"No, it's not. Maybe I pissed you off in there —" She scoffed, but he pushed on, "but there's someone out there watching you and we don't know what their intentions are. You need to be safe right now."

"I'm with almost a dozen giant-sized league players, Finn. I couldn't be safer. And you're coming, right?" She flashed him a sunny smile, but it didn't reach her eyes. "You won't let anything happen to me."

"I'd never let anything happen to you," he swore, his voice gravel. "But we can't predict—"

"I'll be fine," she interrupted, as Dom's deep voice floated through the glass doors announcing the arrival of their taxis. "Don't worry about it." She patted his cheek like he was a goddamned *teddy bear* and swished inside. Frustration boiled inside him, churning his gut.

"Yo, Charming, you're coming with, yeah?" Rangi popped his head out of the sliding glass door.

"Yeah," Finn ground out. "I'm coming." *And if one of you touches her wrong, I'll break your fingers off.*

Cara was pissed. Angry, yes, but mostly boozed, and funnily enough, the more she drank, the less angry she became. So she kept doing it. The beers at Clare and Manu's had been a helpful head start and by the time half the forward pack of the Auckland Knights had refilled her wineglass, she was having a bloody good time, feeling deliciously floaty as she danced. Not drunk, but definitely incapable of operating a motor vehicle. The club they'd ended up at played a plethora of early 2010s bangers and she bumped and ground her way through the songs of her misspent youth as well as she could while surrounded by a circle of Knights players who seemed determined to stop any other patrons reaching her and equally determined not to be her own personal strip poles. They danced with her, sure, hips swaying, hands on her waist, but the slightest accidental brush of her arse against one of them and she was handed off to the next one. *No mixed signals here,* they seemed to say as a collective. *Friends only.*

Meanwhile, her *best* friend propped up the bar, glaring at her as if she'd planned this deliberately to fuck him off. Maybe she had, a little. Maybe after half a decade of friendship and three weeks of overwhelming lust and orgasms that had blown her mind, maybe she was hoping to hear that she'd made a little more of an impression when they'd first met. Between that and the car thing, Finn was doing a damn fine job of convincing her she was more of a convenient fuckdoll than someone he actually wanted to be with. The man sent out more mixed signals than a malfunctioning power line.

Smart, he'd said, and everyone knew in your early twenties that was just code for ugly.

Well, she *was* smart. Too smart to fall in love with someone with his reputation, even if he was sweet and funny and said things that melted her poor pathetic heart and spent his nights doing Sudoku and reading non-fiction instead of hitting clubs and banging groupies like everyone thought. That's probably why he looked so angry now, probably wishing he was at home with a book on the history of native flora rather than this dark den with its sticky floors and Pitbull counting to four in Spanish over the speakers.

She snickered at the thought and stumbled a little. Zac Fearon wrapped his arm around her. Zac was tall and built and smelled excellent, but not the scent of grass and D&G that she craved.

"You good?" He shouted the words into her ear.

She shook her head sadly. "You don't smell like Finn."

"Thank God for that." He looked down at her unsmilingly. This was not a surprise. Zac never smiled. She thought she'd seen it once, when he scored the winning try in the grand championship the season before last, but had convinced herself it must have been a mirage.

She scowled at him. "You wish you smelled like him. He smells amazing."

Zac rolled his eyes. "Okay, Cara. Whatever you say. You want to go over there and sniff him?"

Kind of. No, no, she had too much pride for that.

"I'm gonna get some air," she yelled over the noise, and he followed her off the dance floor like a good little bodyguard, but the instant she was out of the mash of people Finn was there to grab her hand and tow her away.

They were outside in the back alley in a heartbeat. It was a nice alley, all things considered. She'd definitely thrown up in worse ones in her student days.

"Are you alright?" She turned to see Finn watching her. His eyes were wary, but there was something else there, a simmering heat. Cara didn't know if it was anger or desire and didn't want to care.

"I'm fine. Why does everyone keep asking that?"

He shrugged a little, moving a fraction closer, and she stepped closer to the block wall, away from the Dumpster.

"This isn't your usual scene."

"I felt like something new." Cara replied tartly and watched his eyes flare in the dim light.

"Did you now?"

"Yup." She popped the P sound, bratty and obstinate.

He moved closer. "You ignoring me is new."

"I feel like it's working for me tonight."

"It's not working for me."

"Try harder."

His laugh was muffled. "Cara, honey, I've never been able to ignore you for a day in my life. I will not start now because you've got your knickers in a twist over nothing."

Something in his voice cracked her open, through the cosy layer of wine and petulance she'd built up since the game of Truth or Dare. Hurt and hunger flooded her in equal measure. *This man.* He was going to ruin her. One way or another, when the dust settled from this, she wouldn't be the same woman. She only prayed she had the strength to walk away before she gave up all of herself for him.

"It's not nothing. You don't get to tell me what to think," she managed, stepping to the side and heading for the door. His hand grabbed her wrist as she passed and they stood there, suspended in time for a moment, her facing the blank cement block wall and him holding her, caught between her desire to prove her independence and her desire for him. Then he moved, positioning himself behind her, his hands linking with hers and placing them on the wall in front of them before leaving them there and skimming up her arms, over her shoulders, down her sides.

"Do you know what I think?" Finn mused, his warm breath sending goosebumps skittering across the back of her neck and shoulders.

"Not much, probably," Cara responded, fighting back the urge to shiver and the humiliating awareness that it had nothing to do with the temperature.

He chuckled darkly in response. "I think you look beautiful." His lips trailed down her neck, leaving sparks in their wake. "I think you dressed up for tonight. You put on this sexy little dress," his hands roamed over her hips, pressing her back against his bulk, her arse cradling the thick ridge of his erection, "and these fuck-hot heels, and you came out looking for somebody to play with."

"So what if I did?" Cara gasped, arching her back. "I'm a grown woman, Finn. I don't need help to find a playmate."

"No, honey, you don't." His voice was a low growl. "But you know what I think? I think you know I'm the only one you should play with, but you came here instead. I don't think I like that."

Every cell in her that wasn't currently weeping for him to stop talking and get inside her resisted that comment. "It doesn't matter what you like," she spat, and he ran one hand up her torso, skimming her breast, to rest lightly at the base of her neck.

"That's where you're wrong." Finn's other hand was under her skirt now, his fingers tracing light patterns on the skin of her inner thigh. The anticipation wrenched tighter in her, coiling deep as the areas he was *so close* to cried out in neglect. "What I like means everything." One thick thigh pushed between hers, spreading her legs wider. "I like the feel of your soft skin under my hands. I like the noises you make when we kiss, a little moan as if I'm good chocolate and smooth Scotch all rolled into one." His hand cupped between her legs, not moving, holding her as she wriggled. "I like the way you keep this pretty pussy covered in plain cotton. It's the perfect packaging for such a sweet treat." His voice dipped lower, the rough timbre sending a shiver through her. "And it is a sweet treat, isn't it, Cara? The way you melt on my tongue like sugar - I'd give up damn near everything to get a fix."

She moaned, a little mewl that belied her desperation. "You want one now?"

"Mmm." Finn ran his nose up her neck, burying it in her

hair, and inhaled deeply. "I want it all the time. I'm never not thinking about the way you taste, the colour and shape of you. But there's something else I want even more at the moment."

"What's that?" *If he says a kebab, I'll murder him.*

He didn't disappoint. One hand dipped between her legs, under the elastic of her cotton underwear. The hand at her neck dropped to cup her breast, a single thumb brushing back and forth against her nipple, sending shockwaves across her skin.

"I want to be inside you. Do you want that too? Do you want me to fill you up here?" A blunt finger toyed at her opening, teasing her nerve endings.

She whimpered, punching her hips forward, trying in vain to work him inside her. She felt him smile against her hair.

"Uh uh uh. Use your words. Is that something you'd like?"

"Yes," she was nearly sobbing in frustration. "Please."

The top of her dress was down in an instant, his hands holding her, squeezing her. "God, Cara, you feel so good."

"Stop fucking around, Finn. Get inside me."

"Greedy girl." His teeth teased her neck, and she bucked, the sensations racing through her like gunpowder, hot and dangerous.

"Jesus, honey. You're killing me." His hands left her breasts, tugging her underwear to her knees, and then one was back to grip at her hip as she fell forward, the jangle of Finn's belt buckle and the rip of foil music to her ears. The cold brick pressed against her cheek, abrading her nipples. It was electric, the combination of the rough surface scraping lightly across her sensitive peaks, the cool air and the warm press of Finn's body behind her. She whimpered and then he was there, shoving in deep where he belonged, filling her, and she cried out in relief.

He paused inside her, buried to the root, his front pressed to her back, and then ever so gently placed a tender kiss on her cheek.

"Finn?" She tried to catch his eye, but he moved, drawing back and pressing forward, the hot, hard length of him lighting her up inside and her head fell towards the wall, cushioned on her arms where they pressed against the cement.

"This is what you need, isn't it?"

"Yes." It *was* what she needed, this perfect boy who had become her ideal man, loving her with his body and soothing her with his mind, the perfect blend of home and heat, offering her comfort even as she craved him.

"Just this," he murmured in her ear as he pumped, the head of his cock dragging across her G-spot, working her higher with the soft croon of his voice. "Just us. You needed me. Nobody else. Just me."

"Just you," she confirmed, too gone to lie to him, to lie to herself. "I only want you."

"You have me. And that's how it's gonna be every day. Just you and me."

"Yes."

"Ahh." He groaned behind her, sliding hot and full between her legs as he spoke. "I can't hold on when you say it. But I will, I will, honey. I'll keep going as long as you need. This cock was made for you. *I* was made for you. Take what you need, Cara, cos you're never getting this from anyone else again. Whenever your pussy needs filling, it'll be me doing it. Hard and rough, slow and tender. Any way you want it, you come to *me*." One arm banded around her stomach, jerking her back on the thick column of his cock, the other slapping down on her ass. Heat bloomed across her from the point of impact, mingling with the dark tingle that built inside, and she choked his name out against the concrete wall as she grasped at the hand holding her to him.

"That's it, honey. Say my name. Tell everyone who makes you feel this good." He licked up her neck and her vision blacked out as he ground the next words into her skin. "Tell everyone whose woman you are."

His hand moved from her ass to her clit and pressed down *hard*. The sensation was enough to send her flying over the edge, her flesh squeezing down on him and he pumped up, up, up into her, whispering praise as she came apart in his arms.

"Oh God," Finn panted, his thrusts jerky and wild as her head fell back against his shoulder, her knees weak. The top half of his body pressing her against the wall while his hips worked her below. "Oh God, Cara, the way you go off around me… it's a fucking dream." He broke off, harsh pants filling the air as he pounded into her, a desperate rhythm that had her tightening around him again as aftershocks trembled through her. Then he pitched forward, shuddering into her, his next words carried to her ears on the back of his strangled roar.

"Marry me."

CHAPTER 13

The words spilled out of him, as bright and uncontrollable as the cum shooting up his dick. They were bad, he knew they were bad, but in some ways it was so good, such a relief to have them out in the world instead of swirling around his head, pressing against his tongue and fighting for release every time she grinned at him, or breathed, or nestled on the couch to read with her bare feet in his lap.

Jesus, the release. He was giddy with it. With having it out in the open. She was his. She'd said so. Finally.

Except, she didn't feel exactly like his in his arms. She felt stiff in a way he'd never felt her before.

"You okay, honey?" He kissed her temple, willing her to relax, to feel the love pouring off him in waves. *It's going to be alright, it's going to be alright.*

"Uh huh," she answered, but her voice was an octave too high and he sighed and drew out of her reluctantly.

She avoided his gaze as she worked her underwear back up her legs and he dealt with the condom, tying it off and tossing it in the nearby Dumpster.

Jesus, an alley. What was I thinking?

He hadn't been, had he? But that didn't make anything he'd said less honest.

"Cara -"

"I think we should go home," she interrupted.

"Together?" He pressed, and she looked up at him. The wariness in her dark eyes was like a knife to his gut, but she nodded.

"Yes. I think…" she hesitated slightly. "I think we probably need to talk about some things. Privately."

Finn nodded. She hadn't said no. She hadn't said yes. She'd said nothing. Static filled his brain and stayed there, a veil through which he made his way back inside to say goodbye to the others, Cara by his side as they made it to the street. The silence stretched between them in the taxi home, thick as taffy, coating everything with a sticky residue. She frowned out the window the entire ride, arms wrapped around herself while Finn watched her out of the corner of his eye, his chest tight with trapped breath as uncertainty snuck in.

Cara was out of the car like a shot when it pulled up in front of the house, through the door before he was out of the vehicle. He found her on the patio through the French doors off the living room, giving Ted the chance to do his business on the nearby grass.

He cleared his throat. "Would you like some water?"

"Yes, please." She nodded without meeting his eyes, and he returned to the kitchen and busied himself fixing two glasses, adding electrolyte powder to his and mixing it in. He hadn't drunk much but already the pounding at his temples threatened to overwhelm him. The backs of his eyes prickled, and he blinked rapidly.

She's not rejecting you. She's not rejecting you. She just doesn't want to marry you.

Fuck, that thought hurt, but he'd been hurt before and he'd survived.

Taking the glasses through to the patio, he handed her one.

"Thanks."

"No problem," he replied stiffly. *Tell me what you want.*

She'd removed her shoes, and now studied her bare feet, wiggling her toes against the polished concrete.

"Did you mean it?" If every one of his senses hadn't been straining towards her, waiting for some kind of sign, he might have missed her question entirely.

"Yes," Finn replied vehemently. "Absolutely."

"It seems sudden."

He let out a hollow laugh as his chest cracked open. "Does it? I've been in love with you since the week I met you, Cara." Her shocked brown eyes met his, and he nodded. "Yeah. The whole time."

"I didn't know," she whispered.

"Believe me, that was painfully obvious."

"But *marriage*?" Her voice strained on the word. "We've lived together for a month. We've been sleeping together less than that. What if we don't work long term? What if I snore and your habit of squeezing the toothpaste in the middle of the tube gets to me and breaks us apart?"

Finn opened his mouth to answer, then paused. He did squeeze the toothpaste out from the middle of the tube. "You've thought about it."

"I've thought about being your girlfriend, but I haven't thought about *us* in a forever kind of way."

She might as well have knifed him in the chest.

"Cara," Finn said, slowly, gesturing towards the glowing interior of the house. "Look at this place. I asked your opinion on every detail when it was being built. You picked half the art on the walls. There's enough room for as many kids as you want. I built this house hoping you'd share it with me one day. That we would raise our family here. When I imagine my forever, you're all I think about."

Shocked eyes met his. She didn't know. Intellectually he'd known she didn't, but fuck it hurt to see the truth written across her face. She opened her mouth, but he held up a hand, stopping her.

"Don't. You don't have to say anything." Frustration huffed out of him. Why hadn't he done this properly? Rose petals and champagne and candlelight. No wonder she was looking at him like he was a stranger. He'd sex-proposed in an alley and dragged her home to dump all his love on top of her like unwanted luggage. He could write a playbook on how not to get the girl with moves like this. But even with that in mind… she hadn't answered.

"I think," Cara started slowly. "I think I'll take Ted for a walk."

"I'll come with you," Finn offered, but she was already shaking her head.

"No. I need to be alone for a while." The pain in her eyes bit at him, because he could see how much it was hurting her to hurt him with her next words. "I need some space."

He knew he should argue, but fuck, that phrase sank into him like a knife, twisting in his chest as all hope gurgled out. He nodded silently and Cara moved past him back into the house. Through the rush in his ears he heard her call for Ted and gather his lead, the thump of her boots as she switched them out for the battered canvas sneakers she kept in the shoe rack, then the front door shut and Finn let himself fall into a chair and buried his head in his hands, grief throbbing a thick beat through him.

In situations like these, no answer was an answer in itself.

~

CARA DRAGGED air into her lungs, trying to wrestle down the panic that swirled inside her as she exited the gate and turned onto the neatly manicured boulevard. Ted's collar tinkled as he trotted beside her and she focused on that as she walked, on the clink and jangle of his registration and the personalised nametag Finn had come home with the week earlier, his cellphone number engraved on the back. He hadn't mentioned finding Ted a new home in weeks. Animal Control hadn't been in contact. And Ted had a brand new bone-shaped tag on his collar with Finn's personal number on it.

Finn wasn't stupid - like anyone in the public eye he attempted to keep his personal information private. As private as one could be when his age and weight flashed on television screens across the nation weekly. The nametag meant one thing. Ownership. Ted was his dog. Part of their family. She stopped under a streetlight. *Their* family. A vision flashed in front of her eyes - Finn stretched out on his couch, bare feet up on the cushions, those blue eyes focused on some kind of boring historical tome. His hair was freshly washed, the sun streaming in through the living room window picking out the gold in the messy strands, a polo shirt stretched tight across his chest and wrapping around his biceps as he absentmindedly stroked a dozing Ted, curled in his lap snuffling his way through a doggie dream.

She was there too. Moving around the kitchen, stirring a pot on the stove - gluten-free pasta maybe, or a coconut curry. Her headphones peeked out from underneath her hair - the country music she liked to cook to, without disturbing Finn as he read.

Then there would be the nights. Twisted sheets, tangled limbs, hot mouths and hotter climaxes. The best sex of her life, no doubt, but the best moments as well, wrapped around each other, their heartbeats echoing in the still of the night, sweet kisses in the morning sun, sharing their bodies and secrets and souls with one another as days slipped into weeks and months slipped into years.

That's it.

Relief rushed through her, validation pushing the air out of her chest on a ragged exhalation. *That's what I want.*

She'd never been surer. Her doubts and fears evaporated as the image built in her head - an imagined approximation of what she knew her life could be if she trusted in Finn - trusted in herself. A glow built in her chest, taking up space where fear and scepticism had lived since she was fourteen; burying their roots deep, insidious vines that had wrapped around her heart and spread outwards, tainting her relationships, poisoning her against any hope in love and polluting the most important relationship in her life.

Love hadn't almost ruined her relationship with Finn. Cara had. Her fear and unwillingness to try were the reasons she was alone on a midnight street instead of wrapped up in the best man she'd ever known, revelling in the joy they brought to each other's lives. She was in love with him. She'd been in love with him for years. She'd just been too scared to admit it.

"God, I'm such an idiot." The words rang out in the dark, clear and true, and Ted let out a whine at her feet in agreement.

"Come on, Ted." Cara tugged his leash gently as she turned. "Let's go home."

The streetlight at the end of the cul-de-sac beside Finn's driveway glowed like a beacon and she hurried towards it eagerly. The soft slap of the soles of her sneakers echoed off the pavement, heralding her way back to her future.

"Cara."

The voice came out of nowhere. Her heart leapt in her chest and she whipped around to face the street again, but there was nobody there. Several parked cars sat like squat sentries around the pavement perimeter, the way they always did in cul-de-sacs, crammed into corners they didn't quite fit into. Wary, she headed towards Finn's driveway, anxious to be within the high walls. Focused as she was on the wrought-iron gate, she failed to notice the man in black who emerged out of the shadows at the edge of the driveway.

"Shit!"

"Don't be scared," Bernard Shaw said softly. "I just want to talk."

Cara hesitated as he slid between her and the gate, effectively blocking her route to safety.

"What would you like to talk about?" Cara struggled to keep her voice at a normal octave. "Is everything alright with Georgie?"

"Cara." Bernard chuckled and every hair on Cara's body stood on end. "You know I'm not here to talk about Georgie."

No shit, you're not. It must be nearly three in the morning and Cara had never once seen Bernard Shaw outside of the preschool gates. But apparently, he'd seen a lot of her. She ran through the notes her stalker had left, the gifts. *Fucking Bernard.* She hadn't even considered him, with his weak chin and mild-mannered countenance.

Cara eyed the driveway behind her stalker's shoulder. She might have a little too much fondness for cheese, but she was a farm girl at heart and Finn had ensured she could run a proper tackle. Perhaps she could make it...

"You look so pretty." Bernard advanced, his eyes lit with a rapturous expression. "You shouldn't dress like that, you know. But it's just me seeing you now. Did you wear this for me? Did you know I would come for you?"

Fuck me sideways. He's properly insane. She took three steps back in quick concession, and Bernard's expression soured.

"Don't do that," he warned. "Don't run away from me. We're perfect together. You know we are."

"You're married, Mr Shaw," Cara reminded him, dropping Ted's lead behind her back. She couldn't make a run for it while holding him. He was a small dog and she needed the element of surprise in her favour. She'd call for him as she went and he'd follow. God, she hoped he followed.

"Lilith doesn't understand me," Bernard pouted. "She's not a good wife, and I've seen you with Georgie. You'll be a much better mother to her." He held out a hand to her. "Come with me and we can tell her together."

Run, Cara's instincts screamed at her, and she obeyed, driving her legs into the asphalt as hard as she could, sprinting at an angle to Bernard's right, eyes pinned on Finn's gate. If she could get in and hit the button to close it, it wouldn't matter what side of the gate her stalker was on. He could be arrested as easily from outside the property as inside. All she needed was to get to the house.

A scream tore from her lungs as he grabbed her, pulling her and lifting until she was up against his chest, her arms trapped. He was surprisingly strong and as much as she struggled, she couldn't get enough momentum with her legs to do more than kick his shins a few times as he hustled her towards the nearest parked car. Ted barked like crazy, jumping around Bernard's legs as he moved until Bernard kicked out and poor Ted flew several feet through the air, landing with a pitiful yelp.

"You arsehole," Cara hollered. "I'll murder you myself, you son of a bitch!"

She fought with every ounce of her strength as Bernard folded her into the back of the SUV but he suppressed her. *Fucker must do jujitsu or something,* she thought as he bent over her and she tried to bite his ear. He reared back and back-handed her across the face with such force her neck snapped back. Darkness danced at the edges of her vision and a sob rose in her throat as cold steel snapped around her wrist.

I'll never be able to tell Finn I love him. He'll never know I would have said yes.

Underneath her, the vehicle rumbled to life, vibrations shaking her sore head and cool dark climbed the sides of her mind, shutting out every speck of light as she clung to her final thought.

He'll never know.

CHAPTER 14

Finn paced his living room, exasperation rolling off him in waves. He should have known better. Cara was a Libra, for Christ's sake, and thanks to her, he actually knew what that meant. She couldn't make an on-the-spot decision to save her life and not only had he proposed out of thin air, he'd told her he'd been in love with her for years, that *he'd built a goddamned house for her* she had no idea about. No wonder she needed space to process everything. And he needed an exorcist because clearly the devil was driving his decision-making tonight.

Left with nothing to do except stew in self-disgust and pray Cara would come home to him, Finn headed to the fridge and pulled out a chunk of Havarti. Maybe if she returned to a cheese plate she'd be inclined to wait until she'd had something to eat before ripping his heart out of his chest and stomping on it. He could use that time to make amends and prevent it from happening at all. On second thought, cheese alone was unlikely to be enough.

I need quince paste.

Digging through the refrigerator shelves, it took him a

few moments to register the sound of a dog whining at the patio doors.

Ted?

Crossing the living area, he could make out Ted's scruffy white-and-brown fur on the other side of the glass. As he got closer, he noticed the red leash still attached to the dog's collar, the other end trailing across the pale concrete.

"Hey, boy." Finn knelt down to scruff Ted's neck. "Where's your mum?"

Ted let out a piercing yelp as Finn ran his hands down the dog's small body and concern thrummed through him. He gentled his touch and tried again, a whisper-light feathering of his fingers over the dog's ribs and Ted's howl almost deafened him.

"Cara?" Finn called, looking out into the darkness. "Are you there?"

The sound of cicadas whistling in the trees reached him, but otherwise there was silence and no sign of Cara.

"Cara?" Panic laced his voice now. "Cara!"

Ted whimpered again, and Finn scooped him up, supporting his hindquarters rather than holding him around the middle. Long strides eating up the floorboards, he made his way to the counter and scooped up his phone, navigating to his contacts and thumbing a call through.

"What?" Denise's voice was groggily murderous, but he didn't bother to apologise.

"Denise? It's Finn. Have you heard from Cara tonight?"

"What?" Fabric rustled in the background. "No, I haven't. She's not with you?"

"She went for a walk with Ted." *Shit, shit, shit.* "We had a fight. She was angry. I thought she might have called you and asked you to pick her up." He swallowed heavily. "Ted's come home without her and he's hurt."

There was a murmur of voices in the background before

Denise spoke again. "Finn? Call the police. Jodie's going to drive me out to your place. We'll talk to them together."

He was choking, his lungs scrabbling for air past the lump in his throat. "Denise, what if he's got her?"

"Call the police, Finn." Denise replied firmly. "And make some coffee. We need them to pay fucking attention this time." She hung up and Finn stood still with the phone to his ear for a moment; the sticky, sickly fear of his youth edged with a new thread of hysteria threatening to overwhelm him until Ted's damp nose nudged at his throat. *The police. Call the police.* Lowering Ted to the floor as gently as he could, Finn flipped open his wallet and pulled out the card Detective Pring had given him the first day they'd met. By the time the detective had taken the details and promised he was on his way, Denise was banging on his front door with her crutches. He'd left the gate open for them, but Jodie must have broken every speed limit possible on the way out to his place.

He settled Denise on the couch, pillows under her bandaged foot, and fetched them coffees while he went over the details.

"Why did she go for a walk at three in the morning?" Jodie asked, and Finn pressed his lips together, unwilling to reveal his monumental fuckup.

"The police are going to ask," Jodie pointed out reasonably, and Finn sighed.

"I asked her to marry me."

Jodie's gasp echoed through the high ceilings, but Denise eyeballed Finn suspiciously.

"You asked her to marry you and she went for a walk?"

"She wanted to think it over," he replied defensively.

"What did you do wrong?"

"Denise!" Jodie gasped, but Denise held a hand up to quiet her fiancée.

"Trust me, love. Cara's not the dramatic type. A proposal already might seem quick but it's not unheard of. If she went off to think about it, it's because something went wrong."

Shame curdled in Finn's gut. "I might have asked her after sex."

"Oof," Jodie muttered.

"Or..." he hesitated, "I might have kind of asked *during* sex."

Jodie made the sign of the cross.

A knock interrupted before he could offer context - not that there was much that would make it sound better - the efficient *rat-a-tat-tat* that belonged exclusively to law enforcement.

Finn let Detectives Pring and Maxwell in, the latter sneaking subtle glances around his entryway as he led them to the living room and pulled the security camera feed onto the giant television on the wall, rewinding an hour or so. They watched the main entrance camera footage in silence as Cara slipped out of the gate as it opened, looking tiny on screen, her sneakers glowing white in the night vision filtered recording. Other rectangles on the screen remained still, none of the small exclamation points in the top left corner indicating movement. The only thing out of place early on a Sunday morning was the love of his life walking out of his place with Ted at her heels.

She strode out of the side of the image and out of his view. Icy fingers clutched at Finn's heart. *What if that's it? What if that's the last time I see her? Walking away from me on a shitty camera feed?* Panic rose again, harder and faster, stealing his breath in sharp claws and he dragged more in, rougher, rougher, *not enough, it's not enough,* fear ratcheting tighter as he struggled to fill his lungs, eyes fixed on the screen where Cara had last been.

Dimly, he was aware of someone rubbing his back, of a

glass of water being shoved into his hand and he drank it unthinkingly, gasping for air as he finished.

"I think he needs to lie down," someone said in the background but Finn didn't listen, didn't acknowledge them, couldn't do anything but stare at the camera feed for the gate where a small exclamation mark icon had popped up in the top left corner.

"Wait, wait." He interrupted the others. "Something's happening."

They fell quiet, attention fixed on the screen where the icon quivered at the top like a warning.

"Someone's there." Finn murmured. "Someone we can't see properly. They must be in the bushes."

A minute or two later, Cara appeared in the bottom corner. Finn watched as she spun around, looking back the way she'd come, then faced the driveway again.

She was coming home. Coming back to me. The knowledge hit him like a truck and he sank to the couch, lifting the remote and adjusting the settings so the gate camera took up the whole screen. Through the blur of the night filter, he watched as a figure came out of the shadows, as Cara retreated and then ran, grappling with the figure who caught her arm, dropping her shoulder like a pro into their midsection trying to foist them off. The silence swelled in his living room as they watched Cara struggle only to be overcome and carried offscreen.

"Okay," Detective Pring cleared his throat. "A clear case of kidnapping. We'll have to take a statement-"

"Wait!" Jodie pointed at the screen. "What's that?"

A dark vehicle swept across the edge of the frame; no lights, a hint of a white bumper sticker visible on the tailgate. Adrenaline thrumming in his veins, Finn lifted the remote and replayed the shot slowly.

"What does that say?" Detective Maxwell moved closer to the screen. "I can't see with the glare of the night lens."

"It says Save Our Seas." Denise answered grimly, and when Finn swung to look at her, he caught the green tinge of her face. "I recognise the car. It belongs to Georgie Shaw's parents."

"Do you have their address?" Finn was already standing, moving towards the counter for his keys.

"I can get it." She pulled her phone out of her pocket and tapped the screen a few times.

"You can't go riding in to get her," Detective Pring warned Finn as Detective Maxwell moved closer to Denise, peering over her shoulder at the phone. "There are procedures to follow."

"Fuck your procedures," Finn snarled. "If you want to stop me, you'll have to beat me there."

"I could arrest you."

"You could try."

"Got it," Denise called. "They live in Ōrākei." She rattled off a street address.

"Stay here," Finn called to her, already running for the hallway that led to the garage. Behind him, he heard Pring curse. "I'll ring you when she's safe."

He threw himself into the Beemer and smashed the button for the garage door opener.

God, please let her be safe.

<h1 style="text-align:center">CHAPTER 15</h1>

*P*ain.

Ugh, so much pain.

It flared behind Cara's eyelids, pulsing outwards, a super-nova of suffering. She breathed deeply through her nose and tried to focus. A hangover and a head trauma all in one. Wasn't she the luckiest girl in town?

She cracked one eye open. A lamp in the corner provided some illumination - enough to make out she was in an average sized room. It looked almost like a hotel, a large bed draped with navy bedding taking up most of the space and a door she presumed led to a bathroom. It couldn't be a hotel though, surely. Someone would have noticed her being carried unconscious to the room if it were. She was five feet ten, for goodness' sake. Panic fluttered in her chest as she took in the rest of the room; a small sitting area with a coffee table and television, a single armchair matching the one she was in, heavy, closed drapes.

The armchair she was in had been pulled over to the radiator, so she could be handcuffed to it without the pesky need for dumping her on the floor. A gentleman's abduction.

Was it still night or had she been out long enough for a new day to dawn?

Has Finn noticed I'm missing? Even under the fine layer of panic coating her like a sheen of sweat, her heart ached for the way she'd left things with him.

But she was alive. Even better, she was conscious. Opening both eyes, she took further stock of her situation, cataloguing any details that might help. She wasn't near any furniture save the chair she was in. There were no signs of phones or laptops — nothing she could use to communicate with, even if she could get to them. The handcuff bit into her wrist and she studied it closely, praying Bernard was stupid enough to buy his handcuffs from a sex shop and there might be a built-in release.

"It's no good."

Cara startled, dropping the cuff from her free hand.

"My brother-in-law is a cop," Bernard continued, hovering in the doorway she'd noticed. Behind him, a mirror reflected the room back at her — a shower, a vanity, a toilet. "You won't get it off without breaking your fingers."

"Are you anticipating breaking my fingers?" Cara fought to keep her voice cool.

Bernard shook his head vigorously. "No, no. I would never hurt you," he claimed vehemently.

"You knocked me unconscious," Cara pointed out.

"That was different," her stalker insisted. "You weren't listening. That's why I brought you here, so we can talk with no interruptions."

Talking beats being murdered. "What would you like to talk about?" She strove for a caring interest even as she used her free hand to pull the fabric of her dress further down her thighs, covering as much of her exposed flesh as possible.

"Us, of course."

"Of course," she forced out. "You, uh, you mentioned something about leaving Lilith?"

"Lilith needs to go," Bernard responded sourly as he crossed the room towards her and Cara suddenly became deeply concerned for Lilith's safety.

"But in a divorce kind of way, right?"

"Of course. What did you think I meant?" Cold grey eyes slid over her and Cara fought back a shiver.

"Divorce. I thought you meant divorce. I was just checking."

"You moved," Bernard said suddenly. "You moved house. Why did you do that?"

Cara swallowed hard. "I was, um, house-sitting. For a friend. He needed his dog looked after."

Bernard's face darkened. "He?"

"He's a friend," Cara protested, the lie thick in her throat. "I have male friends."

He was already shaking his head. "You don't understand. Men can't be friends with you. They'll always want you. The temptation…"

He moved closer, reaching out to stroke her hair, and a shudder of revulsion worked sharply through her.

Bernard smiled indulgently. "It's hard, isn't it? Being so close and not able to touch each other yet? Don't worry, my love," he crooned and tears pricked at Cara's eyes. "I won't make a whore of you. We'll tell Lilith together when she wakes up. She can pack her things while we take Georgie out for breakfast and then tonight…" His eyes glowed with the alternate reality he wove. "Tonight, it will only be the two of us. Like it should have been all along. I knew it from the moment I saw you."

Cara swallowed, her mind racing. Bernard stood over her, touching her hair, and her scalp crawled. If she got out of here, she was cutting it all off.

"Mr Shaw?"

"Bernard," he corrected. "We're together now, you should call me by my first name."

"Right." Cara forced a smile. "Of course. Um, Bernard, do you think you could please uncuff me?"

He stepped back and studied her, his small mouth pulled tight in suspicion. "You tried to run from me."

"I didn't understand what was happening then," Cara said. "But you've explained it to me now. I need to use the bathroom," she lied. She was so tense she'd likely never pee again, but bathrooms had windows and she needed to get the fuck out of this place before this madman pulled out a wedding dress and carved a smile into her face.

"Only to use the bathroom," Bernard insisted. "Then back in the chair. I can't have Lilith seeing you before we tell her."

So, I'm at the Shaws' house. Having that one piece of the puzzle solved helped steady her.

"Of course," Cara assured him. "That makes sense." The only other door in the room was to her left. Bernard would need to stand on that side to uncuff her; his body would block her path. If the bathroom door locked, it would give her more time, but the window might be locked or too small to escape through. Frazzled strands of fear threatened to overwhelm her. *What should I do? Which way do I go?*

Bernard pulled a small silver key from his pocket and moved to her left, to the wrist that was cuffed. Watching her carefully, he unlocked it and loosened the steel casing from her wrist. Cara cradled it against her chest, running the fingers of her right hand over the red imprints the cuff had left behind.

"Thank you," she said quietly. "May I go to the bathroom now?"

Bernard nodded and took a step back as she rose and tested her legs. They were a little wobbly, and she moved back and forth on the spot gently, eyes downcast, the picture of submission until she got her bearings and then she exploded. She shunted the heel of her right hand into Bernard's nose as hard as she could, then ran without waiting to see if it had done any damage. She was almost at the door when he caught her ankle, pulling her onto the carpet, her fingers scrabbling at the wood as she went.

So close. So close.

"You fucking bitch," Bernard snarled, his breath hot on the back of her legs as he tried to climb up her. "All I did was love you. You don't deserve a nice guy like me, but I'll show you. You'll see." He flipped her over, his bloody face rearing back to avoid her flailing fists as true terror streamed through her for the first time. She thrashed like a fish on a wire, fighting for her life, the momentum moving her across the floor as she kicked up and out every time he moved towards her. Blood rushed in her ears, blocking out everything except the overwhelming voice screaming at her to survive. Her head hit something, and she threw one arm up to protect herself, only to find her hand wrapped around the tall corner lamp. Kicking out again to give herself some space, she jackknifed up and swung it with all her might. The metal base pole hit Bernard's shoulder, and she swung again, quickly, no time for a big build-up. This time it made contact with the side of his bloodstained face and she leapt to her feet as he staggered sideways, her stunted hockey career coming to the fore as she gripped the lamp base in two hands and swung, a perfect upward arc that connected beautifully in a shower of broken glass, sinking them into semi-darkness.

"You motherfucker," she screamed, swinging again, connecting again, her fear and panic channelling itself into pure fury. "I'll kill you."

She pulled back for another hit when someone grabbed

her from behind, trapping her arms and the lamp in front of her.

"Let go of me," she yelled, kicking at the air.

"Ms Holt, this is Detective Pring." The voice beside her ear was steady and firm. "I'm going to release you so I can assist my colleague with arresting Mr Shaw. Please do not attempt to hurt him further. Or me," he added.

Cara stilled, and he lowered her to the ground.

Detective Maxwell crouched above Bernard. As Cara watched, she knelt heavily on the general area of his kidneys and handcuffed his wrists behind his back.

Good. I hope he has to piss into a bag for the rest of his life.

The violence behind the thought jolted her and tears ran unchecked in hot tracks down her cheeks. Shaking, she backed out of the room, fumbling her way down the stairs in front of her and outside. She'd been in a studio above a garage - she could see the main house ahead of her in the navy-pink blush of the morning sky. The Oamaru stone walls were cold in the early morning chill and she leaned against one, ignoring the shivers wracking her body as she gulped in deep breaths of crisp air and finally - *finally* - let go. She sobbed into the quiet peace of the morning, pain and fear leaching out into the air so loudly she almost didn't hear her name.

"Cara!"

She opened her eyes. There, through the film of tears, was Finn. He sprinted towards her, backlit by the dawn sky, strong arms wrapping around her the instant he got close enough, supporting her as her knees gave way in relief. Cara clutched at him as she wept and he rocked her gently, dropping kisses across her shoulder, her neck, her cheek, wherever he could reach.

"You're okay," he murmured, over and over. "You're okay, honey. You're okay."

Slowly her sobs died down to sniffles, and she raised her head from his shoulder, tilting her neck to look into his eyes. His own pain was there, mingled with relief and a love so deep and true she couldn't believe she'd never noticed it there before.

"You found me."

He exhaled heavily and pressed his forehead to hers.

"Denise found you. I was the one stupid enough to lose you in the first place."

"No," Cara shook her head vehemently. "You can't lose me. Not ever. I was coming back to you. I was coming back to tell you I was sorry, and I was wrong. I should have said yes as soon as you asked."

"You're not scared of loving me?"

"The only thing that scares me is the idea of living without you. You haven't given me reason to doubt you before. Why would I start now?"

She kissed him, a hard kiss to wash away the vileness of everything she'd been through since their lips last met.

Someone cleared their throat nearby and Cara pulled back reluctantly. Lilith Shaw stood by the garage staircase in a feather-trimmed robe, one hand fluttering by her neck.

"I'm so sorry," the other woman said, her face drawn. "I'm so sorry. I had no idea."

"I know," Cara dredged up a smile. She might not particularly like Lilith, but there was no doubt in her mind the woman was as shocked by her husband's actions as Cara. "I know you didn't. It's okay."

Lilith promptly burst into tears. "What am I going to tell Georgie?"

Cara was saved from answering by Detective Maxwell who came to inform them that Bernard was about to be escorted down and they should vacate the driveway if they didn't want to see him. She mentioned he was bleeding heavily from the face and Lilith answered, "good," with a level of savagery that both impressed and heartened Cara.

"I'm taking Cara home," Finn informed the detective roughly.

"We need her at the station to make a statement," Detective Maxwell replied.

"You can take it at my place tomorrow," he snapped. "She needs to rest."

For once, his protective nature acted as a balm, and she relaxed against his chest, secure in the knowledge she didn't need to make any decisions, that after the biggest battle of her life there was someone there to fight the smaller skirmishes on her behalf. Love, Cara decided, as Finn bundled her into his SUV, changed everything.

CHAPTER 16

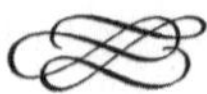

ne month later.

THE LIGHTS SHONE down on the emerald grass of Knights' Stadium. Across the field, men lay scattered, their breath misting in the night air, hazy halos that spoke of their effort in battle.

Cara didn't have eyes for any of it. All she could see was her boyfriend striding towards her, powerful thighs bunching as he ate up the distance between them, sandy hair spiked, blue eyes electric with victory.

"Whoooo!" Izzy cheered beside her. "Let's go, Chalmers."

Their parents' imminent divorce and Bernard Shaw's upcoming trial had brought Izzy back to Aotearoa, along with a confession to Cara that she was disillusioned with the life of a nanny and keen to try a different direction. It's why they were in the stands - front row seats - rather than the box. Izzy had insisted on attending the first official game of the season like a real fan.

"Not like you and the WAGs," she'd told Cara. "Let's do it properly. We'll eat hot donuts and drink warm beer, and yell at the referee."

Cara was glad she'd agreed as the players filed off the field. It was certainly quicker than waiting in the after-match room for them to shower and dress and finish their recap.

"You're just waiting to smell him, aren't you?"

Zac Fearon stood in front of their section of the stands, headgear in hand, dark hair mussed, dirt and blood streaking his tanned face.

"You know it," Cara responded. "Best part of my day."

Zac rolled his eyes, and she grinned. "This is my sister, Isabel," she said, gesturing to Izzy, whose gaze was firmly fixed on some point in the distance. "Izzy, this is Zac."

Zac looked at Izzy, and his eyebrows jumped. "Your sister?" he echoed.

Izzy's eyes slid to the Knights player. "That's right," she replied coolly, startling Cara. Izzy got on with everyone. "Zac, was it?" her sister continued.

A pink flush crept up Zac's neck, but he didn't drop his eyes from Izzy's. "That's right," he replied evenly. "Isabel, was it?"

"Sure is." Izzy bared her teeth at Zac in a feral approximation of a smile.

Before Cara could ask what was going on, Finn reached them. He grinned up at her and her heart swooped. Izzy and Zac's weirdness melted away as she took in the sight of the man she loved, flushed with triumph. Finn had always been gorgeous, but looking at him now was like staring into the sun.

Mine. All mine.

"Good win, Cap," Zac pronounced, clapping Finn on the shoulder.

"Thanks, Fearon. You staying for the aftermatch?" Finn didn't take his eyes off Cara.

"Can't. Got something I need to take care of at home," Zac responded. "I'll catch you at training on Monday."

Finn nodded and reached out a hand for Cara. "Climb over. I want you down here with me."

It was only about eight feet from their row to the field below. Cara swung her legs over the section railing and jumped, wrapping her legs around Finn's waist as he caught her.

"Hi," he said as he settled her against him, tipping his head back to rub the tip of his nose against hers.

"Hi back," she whispered. "Good game."

"Glad you liked it."

"I'll catch you later, Cara," Izzy called from above them. "Catch, Chalmers!" She tossed a small paper bag at him, which he plucked out of the air before returning his hand to its rightful place on the curve of her rear. "I saved you a donut."

Finn acknowledged her with a tilt of his head, his eyes still on Cara. Around them, the stadium emptied quickly, fans streaming out. Patches of empty red seats bloomed and connected until a scarlet ring surrounded them. Finn loosened his hold and Cara slid down his big body, pressing tight against him in a way that made him groan, that familiar scent of sweat, grass and cologne teasing her nostrils.

As if reading her mind, Finn pressed his face against her neck and inhaled.

"You smell good," he murmured, the tickle of his breath making her squirm.

"So do you."

He chuckled lightly. "I just played eighty minutes of rugby league. I probably smell terrible."

"You smell like the captain of a winning team."

"Yeah?" He smiled tenderly at her as he pulled back, linking their hands and tugging her towards the nearest set of goalposts. "You like the smell of success on me?"

"I like everything about you."

They strolled hand in hand towards the Knights' try line - the try line Finn had crossed twice earlier in the evening to secure his team the victory - and sat down, legs stretched out in front of them. Overhead, the goalposts rose like sentries, reaching high towards the sky that bled from periwinkle to navy in the dying light of the summer sun. A handful of stars winked down at them as Cara rested her head on Finn's shoulder.

"A perfect night," she sighed, watching as the lights of a plane blinked overhead, moving slowly across the twilight vista.

"Almost," Finn said.

She tilted her head and shot him a questioning look. "How would you make it better? Should I have brought Ted?" she teased.

Finn smiled, his free hand tapping an uneven beat on the grass next to him.

"As much as I've grown to love Ted, it's probably better he stays home on game days. I don't need the team distracted by his fancy kerchiefs when they should focus on the opposition."

Ted had become something of a team mascot since his injury. Cara had first brought him along to a team run after the vet appointment where he was declared fully recovered from his bruised ribs. Everyone adored him, and most had gifted him tiny doggie outfits designed to humiliate Finn on their daily walks. Cara's favourite was a rhinestone encrusted Elvis ensemble, courtesy of Dom McQueen.

"Plus," Finn's voice lowered. "I love it when it's only you and me."

Cara sighed contentedly. "Me too." They'd been almost inseparable since that morning on the Shaw's driveway. She'd officially moved in immediately, handing in her notice at her flat in Epsom and hauling her meagre belongings across the bridge to the North Shore in her shiny new SUV, now registered in her name. Izzy had taken over the remainder of her lease on the flat. Cara's kidnapping had clarified her priorities in stark relief - she hadn't objected to the car again, realising her refusal only hurt Finn. That he saw it as another rejection of the love he offered.

My brave man.

In the last few weeks, he'd told her more about growing up with his parents than in all the time they'd known each other. It was like a dam had cracked, and once he was sure she loved him, he let all of his past pain come spilling out. Cara's heart ached for all he'd endured. In return, he'd wrapped his thick arms around her as she processed the news of her parents' divorce. Linda had kicked Steve out finally. Not because of his infidelity, which was long-reaching, it turned out. God knew when he'd found the time to run the farm. But rather, because of Linda's newfound knowledge he'd asked Cara to keep it a secret that ill-fated day when she was fourteen. It seemed Linda might have loved Cara's father, but she loved Cara more. She'd been furious to learn his actions had hurt Cara, and he'd amplified that hurt by shouldering her with a half-lifetime of guilt and secrecy to protect himself.

She and Finn were both products of their parents' failure to protect them, it turned out, but together they were learning to let their pasts go and focus only on their future.

She couldn't be happier.

Finn let go of her hand, rolling from his seated position onto his knees to face her.

"You asked me how I could make this night better," he

said slowly, and she grinned up at him, struck by his beauty, his sweetness, the whole messy, vulnerable perfection of him. Her very own Prince Charming. "There is one thing," he continued, taking a deep breath through his nose.

"Cara, I asked you this once already, but I didn't do it right. I was thinking about me, about what I wanted. And the truth is, all I've ever wanted is you. You've been the sunshine in my life since the day we met. Every beat of my heart has been for you. I tried not to love you, I swear I did, but I might as well have tried not to breathe." He reached into the crumpled donut bag.

"You're my best friend, Cara Holt, and the greatest love I've ever known. You're my family, the family I chose for myself, and it would be the greatest honour of my life if you would choose me too." He pulled a ring out of the bag, a single brilliant cut diamond, bezel-set on a platinum band. "Will you marry me?"

Cara's heart leapt, love swelling in her chest. Here he was, taking a chance. Making himself vulnerable once more in the name of love, but he didn't have to worry about being rejected. Not by her. Not ever.

"Of course." She rose on her knees too, throwing her arms around him. "Of course I will." She peppered his face with kisses, until he caught her lips, kissing her slow and deep. A promise. A vow. A benediction.

"I love you," he exhaled, brushing another kiss against her forehead, then another.

"I love you too, Finn Chalmers. In fact," Cara smiled. "I have something to show you."

"After you put the ring on," he said. "Do you like it? You can get something else."

"Stop." She cupped his face in her hands, running a thumb over the stubble of his cheek. "It's perfect."

He smiled, relief etched into his face. "You're perfect." He removed her left hand from his face and slid the ring on her finger. She stared down at it, sparkling under the floodlights. It felt… weighty. Important. The sheer rightness of it almost knocked her off balance.

"What did you want to show me?"

Cara tore her eyes from the ring, everything it symbolised making her reach for her jeans pocket to pull out her phone.

"It was supposed to wait until we got home," she told him, unlocking the screen. "But I took a picture before I left. I want to show you now. I want you to know."

Turning her phone to face him, she saw the moment he realised. The moment he understood. The photo on her screen showed Ted, tongue out, face blurry because he'd moved as she hit the button, but there on his collar was a note, in perfect focus.

Will you marry my mummy?

Finn's eyes shone when they met hers again. "You're proposing as well?"

Cara nodded, nerves clogging her throat even now with his ring on her finger.

"You hadn't mentioned it again since the alley." He winced at the reminder. "I wasn't sure if you still wanted to. But I do. I wanted to say yes that night." She reached out and grasped his hand, clutching it to her chest. Her ring glinted in the fading light as the stadium's lights dimmed. "You've never been loved the way you should have, Finn, and that breaks my heart. If you let me, I'll spend every day for the rest of our lives showing you how much you mean to me. Loving you as hard as I can. Helping you build the family you deserve. I want to marry you. I want to have children with you. Neither of us will ever be perfect, but we're perfect together. I choose you, this, us. Will you marry me too?"

He was nodding, his blue eyes swimming with unshed tears.

"I will. I'll marry you, Cara. I'm dying to marry you." He kissed her hard. "Let's do it next week."

Joy bubbled up in Cara, spilling out of her mouth in a laugh. "Soon," she promised. "We'll do it soon. But for now, let's celebrate."

"You want to go out? I need to change," Finn pulled at the Knights jersey sticking to his skin.

Cara shook her head. "That's not what I was thinking." She lowered herself down until her back pressed against the grass, tugging at his top to bring him down with her, the familiar weight of him a balm to her soul.

"You've already scored twice on this field tonight. Come on, Charming," she licked his neck and he shivered. "Let's make it a hat trick."

THE END

Turn over for a sneak peek at Izzy and Zac's story,
Two Can Play That Game.

SNEAK PEEK

"Come on," Isabel Holt's older sister pleaded. "You're great at it."

"I'm great at lots of things," Izzy shrugged. "Baking. Charity runs. Blow jobs. I don't do those for just anyone either."

"Zac isn't just anyone. He's one of Finn's teammates!"

"He's an arsehole, is what he is."

The man in question cleared his throat. "I can hear you."

"I know," Izzy snapped. "That's why I said it."

SEE MORE of Zac and Izzy in **Two Can Play That Game** available for preorder now.

ABOUT THE AUTHOR

Award winning author Courtney Clark Michaels has been reading and writing romance since she first pilfered a novel out of her mother's bedroom at the tender age of thirteen. While her newly discovered writing hobby didn't endear her to her teachers, it did make Maths more interesting for her friends. Ironically, after gaining degrees in Criminology and English, Courtney now teaches high school students and spends a fair bit of time bemoaning their off-task behaviour. Karma is indeed a bitch. Courtney's passion for writing strong, independent heroines and smart, sexy men is equal only to her passions for travel, online shopping and patting other people's dogs. She is lucky enough to live in the heart of New Zealand's winemaking region with her own alpha man, a few gorgeous children and a hyperactive poochon named Kevin.

More books by Courtney

Someone Like You - FREE to newsletter subscribers here or sign up to my newsletter by visiting www.courtneyclarkmichaels.com

Pregnant by the Prince - available at Amazon and free in Kindle Unlimited here or ask for it at your local bookstore or library.

Rooming with Royalty - available at Amazon and free in

Kindle Unlimited here or ask for it at your local bookstore or library.

Protecting His Princess - available at Amazon and free in Kindle Unlimited here or ask for it at your local bookstore or library.

Christmas in Paradise - available at Amazon and free in Kindle Unlimited here or ask for it at your local bookstore or library.

facebook.com/courtneyclarkmichaels
twitter.com/c_clarkmichaels
instagram.com/courtneyclarkmichaels_author

ACKNOWLEDGMENTS

All books require a collective effort to get them across the finish line, and that is especially true of Game Changer. This book was written in cafés, edited in airports and submitted from hospital. My thanks to everyone who provided me with support, snacks, electrical outlets and Internet access in the process of bringing Finn and Cara's story to life.

My biggest supporters continue to be my family, who give me the time and grace to get these stories out of my head and onto the page. My husband Fetu first introduced me to rugby league and I'd like to thank him for his expertise over the years as I've learned to enjoy sports a little more, along with Ella and Kade Poki for their time answering questions about the private side of pro sports. A special shout out to Andie Wood, whose generous donation in the Dissent campaign to support abortion access in the United States provided us with the name Ted for Finn and Cara's dog.

As always, I couldn't do this without my writing groups, the Blenheim ladies, and the Wordmakers, and especially Barbara DeLeo who has been such a generous source of knowledge, talent and support since the start of my career. Thanks to Kate and Sally for their thoughtful notes and passion for this project and to Ray Collins and Phillipa Kitchin who consistently make my writing sharper and better through their skillful editing. And to you, dear reader! Thanks for taking a chance on a new series with me. I hope you become as big a fan of the Auckland Knights as I am.

9 780047 361541 3